TEST OF LOVE . . .

"Could you close the shop tomorrow, do you think? Permanently?" Robert said suddenly.

Anne's first reaction was pain. Then, shocked, she asked: "Why ever would I do that?"

"I could find a proper job for you . . . move you into a proper environment. My mother would see to it that you bought the right clothes, met the right people . . ."

Anne said—she couldn't help it: "You ask a lot, Robert."

"Some would say I'm offering a lot," he countered gently.

But inside Anne rebelled: Why in the world did she have to prove she was *worthy* of him?

PUT PLEASURE IN YOUR READING
Larger type makes the difference
This EASY EYE Edition is set in large, clear type—at least 30 percent larger than usual. It is printed on scientifically tinted non-glare paper for better contrast and less eyestrain.

This Love To Hold

Norma Newcomb

VALENTINE BOOKS

NEW YORK

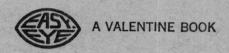 A VALENTINE BOOK

THIS LOVE TO HOLD

Valentine Books are published by
PRESTIGE BOOKS, INC., 18 EAST 41ST STREET
NEW YORK, N.Y. 10017

Chapter One

On Thursday morning the telephone was rung an hour earlier than usual by the paraplegic owner and operator of the Santa Fe Rise and Shine Company. The fellow said as cheerily as ever, 'Rise and shine, Miss Hendlay—it's a *great* morning." But he was human enough to be made uneasy by the unusual. "Miss Hendlay," he asked worriedly, "you did say to ring you at six, didn't you? It's right here on my board."

"Yes."

"Well, I'm glad to hear that, Miss Hendlay. I didn't know if my wife sort of goofed."

"But you're wrong about the morning," Anne told him. "It's impossible for any morning to be a *great* morning at six o'clock."

"Ah, it'll grow on you, Miss Hendlay. Take a real big look at that sunrise!"

Anne pronged the handset, and she did take a

look. Unimpressed, she then closed the bedroom draperies and switched a lamp into high-power glare. The glare disturbed Mona Yates. Rolling over in a badly rumpled bed, Mona protested: "It's your agony, darling; not mine." Anne left the light on, though, reasoning that Mona's punishment ought to fit the crime. "You got me into this mess," she reminded Mona. "If I'm to go to jail, you should at least kiss me goodbye on the paddy-wagon step."

Mona sat up, rubbed her eyes and tried unsuccessfully to stifle a yawn. "Walter said," she argued, "that there's no possibility you'll go to jail."

"Lawyers have guessed wrong before. Do forgive my goof, the lawyer said, as they electrocuted his client."

The telephone rang again.

Robert Lund.

Sounding tired, Robert asked, "I don't suppose that you've changed your mind, Anne?"

"I'm afraid not, Robert. Not that it matters, really. According to Walter Sward, there's no possibility I'll go to jail."

Her tone, carefully gay, offended his concept of propriety. "It isn't that amusing, you know," he rebuked her. "You've upset a lot of people."

Anne wondered why she bothered with him. She had about as much chance of becoming Mrs. Robert Lund as she had of becoming an Indian-handicrafts buyer for Blumberg Variety Stores, Incorporated. In fact, she thought gloomily, she probably had no chance of becoming either.

Robert misunderstood her silence. "Oh, it's quite all right," he said generously. "I forgive you. People sometimes put on bravado at a time like this. I know what I'm talking about. The other day I had to discharge a typist. She was competent, but the wart on her nose displeased one of my major clients. Well, that young lady put on a very gay show of not caring, but—"

"Robert, you *didn't* fire a person for such a reason!"

The silence was long. Then he said soothingly, "Let's take one thing at a time, dearest. Right now, it's your emergency that concerns me. And I think that I've worked out an honorable compromise."

"There's nothing indecent about those statues," Anne said. "They're satire, and that's all they are."

"According to many fine people, Anne, those statues are indecent . . . obscene. Suppose Judge Langley agrees with those people?"

"Go to any swimming pool in the city, Robert, and you'll see women wearing as little clothing."

Across the bedroom, Mona gestured wildly at the alarm clock. Anne nodded, but Robert didn't

7

give her a reasonably good opportunity to hang up.

"The compromise I've worked out," Robert said deliberately, "gives each faction at least a fragment of what he wants. Mrs. Staunton will display the statues for a month in her salon, so Tom Zimmerman will have every opportunity to show his work to people who buy. At the same time, the people who've been offended by those statues will have the satisfaction of seeing them removed from display in the patio of the Indian Arts Shoppe. See?"

Anne drew a deep breath.

"No," Robert said, as if sensing her thought, "I'm not a genius. I sat up all night working this out. To be frank, I don't care a nickel about Tom Zimmerman's work, or even about his rights as an artist. I do care about you, however. So there you are. I've talked with Mrs. Staunton, and I've talked with the leaders of those different women's groups. If you're willing to compromise, the thing is settled."

Anne said, touched: "That was kind of you, Robert. Thanks."

"Well, a man does these things from time to time. When are you seeing Sward?"

"He's due at seven. Glory, I'd better dress!"

"All right. Discuss the compromise with him. Tell him I've already checked with Judge Langley.

Judge Langley told me quite unofficially that if the statues are exhibited in a bona fide museum, there's not a thing anyone can do to terminate their display. Judge Langley also told me quite unofficially that in the long run, Tom Zimmerman will benefit from such a display in such a setting."

Anne said impulsively, "As a matter of fact, I agree. Do you accept telephone kisses?"

But he laughed and hung up, did Mr. Robert Lund, before Anne could pucker her lips. Anne turned from the telephone with mixed emotions. She relayed the news to Mona. Inclined to swagger somewhat because of this evidence that Robert cared, she elaborated happily: "I may marry that man one of these days. Of course, his family's a problem. It's been so long since they've had a working girl in that family that they think I'm some kind of freak. But they're all right, you understand. They just have some prejudices to get rid of."

"You'd better shower and dress."

"But why? All our problems are solved! We compromise, everybody gets something, and I stay out of the clink."

Anne showered and dressed, though. Now that she was up, she thought, she might as well stay up. Directly after the chat with Walter, she'd go to the shop and write another long letter to Mr. Solomon Blumberg in Denver. This time, by golly, she'd

9

threaten her old boss. And if the threat didn't persuade him to try her out as a buyer, she'd darned well telephone him collect!

Meanwhile—

At seven o'clock, lovely and assured in a brown tweed suit, Anne opened the door to Walter's ring and took him into the dining room. Mona had breakfast ready to serve, and the lawyer smiled and sat down, in high good humor. "If anyone around here is looking for a husband," he said, "here I am. I don't like restaurant breakfasts."

"Anne's marrying Robert Lund," Mona informed him. "Robert Lund may not know it, but that's a mere technicality."

Walter was interested. "That's the broker? Scion of the old family?"

"Well, he just dabbles in stocks and bonds to keep busy," Mona cracked. "One has to do something, you know."

Walter shot a keen glance at Anne. "You're out of your league," he opined. "Anyway, don't marry him for a while, okay? I have to sue him, you see, and I'd hate to sue your husband."

"Oh?"

"That guy actually fired a typist because she has a wart on her nose."

"Well," Anne defended him, "the wart bothered an important client. I suppose it was either

10

fire the girl or lose a big account. What would you have done, Walter?"

"What I plan to do," Walter said, "is sue that man for a quarter of a million dollars. But that's another day. Now let's get down to the little problem we have right now. We're to meet Judge Langley in the patio of the Indian Arts Shoppe at eight o'clock. You don't say a word to the judge until he asks you a question. If he tells you to get rid of the statues, you then say very mildly that you respectfully refuse to obey his order on the grounds that there's no law in Santa Fe that forbids a person to own or display works of art. Catch? Play everything coolly, even casually."

Anne told him about the compromise Robert had worked out. Walter listened attentively, fork poised between carp-like mouth and plate, beady black eyes fixed on her face. When she'd finished, he chuckled. "Highly irrelevant," he announced. "The issue here is whether a citizen and taxpayer of Santa Fe does or doesn't have the right to own and display a work of art. I couldn't care less about the art-versus-obscenity matter. How do you define either? But I do care about civil liberties. That's why I'm in this case. If the mob can force you to junk those statues today, it can force you to junk your other rights tomorrow."

"Still," Anne said, "I'm a businesswoman, Walter. Frankly I displayed those statues to help

11

Tom Zimmerman. I certainly didn't expect to become involved in a furor like this. And now that I have a chance to extricate myself from the furor gracefully—well, why not?"

"Very simple," Mona said. "Don't forget, darling, that I know Mrs. Staunton very well. That salon of hers is just a tax dodge—a little thing she's set up so that she can cut her taxes by putting a lot of money into art objects. It's very clever. Say her gross income is half a million dollars a year. The taxes on such an income are enormous. But she can write off all expenses incidental to operating and stocking that salon. Catch?"

"Still—"

"She'll bury Tom's statues in a room nobody'll ever enter—or hardly anybody. So you may be out of the mess, but Tom won't be helped."

Walter finished his coffee and rose. A stocky, moon-faced man, he looked at his Accutron wristwatch and said, "I advise you to forget Lund's compromise. But it's up to you, Anne."

Along about then, Anne grew cross with herself. She ought to have known better than to let Mona talk her into displaying those statues! They'd been a headache from beginning to end. She didn't even like the things. Men had no right to satirize women as Tom had satirized them with those statues. And anyway, the statues weren't at all related to Indian arts. That was her specialty. She ought to have concentrated on her specialty!

Walter said intensely, "The principle I'm fighting for, Anne, is important. There's too much control these days—all the way down the line from top to bottom. If people don't like something, they holler for a law or for the police or even use the law of the mob. You have every legal right to display those statues. They're not immoral in any sense of the word. So to quit now, after all this fuss—well, Lund will admire you, I'm sure. Why not? He's the fellow who fired a typist because she has a wart on her nose."

Anne asked, not wanting to, "The principle is that important? A thing like this could ruin my business. What about that?"

"Would I be risking my professional standing in the community if I didn't think the principle worth fighting for?"

Anne sighed and rose. She got her handbag and went out to Walter's ridiculously gaudy Cadillac convertible. As they drove through the quiet streets to the ancient quarter of the city, she had a sudden conviction that this was the most fatal ride she'd ever taken in her life. Robert would be furious! Robert's family would look down their collective noses and ask, "Well, what did you expect of a working girl?" And suppose the threatened boycott of the Indian Arts Shoppe were

13

made a reality? Old Sol Blumberg in Denver would laugh at the business proposition she'd made.

But she kept these thoughts and fears to herself, head high, as always, smile softly perky, as they swept by the State Capitol Building and made the righthand turn to cross the Santa Fe River. It gave her a queasy sensation when she spotted a tall, austere-looking man in funeral black pacing to and fro before the patio entrance to the Indian Arts Shoppe, but she managed to contain that reaction, too. After Walter had introduced her to Judge Langley, she unlocked the wrought-iron gate and led the men into the patio. Remembering Walter's admonition to say not a word until the judge asked her a question, she struck off alone to a wrought-iron bench, while the two men stepped around the shallow ornamental pool for closer looks at the five gleaming, copper-foil statues. Studying the monstrous creations for the umpteenth time, Anne found it incredible that anyone could call them obscene. Tom hadn't even exaggerated the bosoms and bottoms overflowing the copper-foil Bikinis. At any poolside these days you could see actual flesh overflowing actual Bikinis. Of course, the real-life hippos in their preposterously skimpy Bikinis were never on display quite as yonder statues were, but they certainly weren't invisible, either. Actually, the only thing wrong with the work, in her opinion, was that Tom had been unnecessarily cruel to satirize the female folly of wearing anything and everything that was "in" lest one be, style-wise, "out." But that, Anne thought, was an entirely different argument.

Judge Langley motioned for Walter to stay put, and then he walked over to join Anne on the wrought-iron bench. He smiled at her pleasantly and easily. "I imagine all this has been a strain for you, Miss Hendley," he said. "It's never easy to be in opposition to society, is it?"

"The odd thing," Anne said frankly, "is that I don't want to be. At twenty-three or twenty-four, what does a human being really know? When I was a teen-ager, I was positive that society was wrong about many things. As I grew older, I learned that society had been right and that I had been wrong. Probably I'm wrong about this, and if I alone were involved, I'd cheerfully take these things to the dump. But Tom Zimmerman happens to be a sincere artist. He's not trying to achieve success through notoriety, scandal. Tom thinks that way about the stupidity of women wearing clothes they're not constructed to wear attractively. And Tom thinks it's a duty of artists to comment about human foibles."

"I predict a hard life for the man, Miss Hendlay. Women don't like to be satirized. Now that

15

I've seen these things, I understand the violence of the opposition."

Anne waited for him to make the fateful decision, to speak the fateful words that would ultimately land her in jail.

Judge Langley chuckled and rose. "Well," he said casually, "I certainly won't issue an injunction to prevent you from displaying those things. It's your business to display art objects of all kinds, and I dare say those things can be called art. Obviously, they're not obscene under any definition of the word that I've read. But my friend Robert Lund won't be happy with you if you exercise your legal right to keep on displaying those statues. Have you thought of that?"

"But a person can't just refuse to help another person, sir, as I'm trying to help Tom and other artists."

He crinkled his forehead. "I'm afraid," he said, "that you'll have a hard life, too, Miss Hendlay. People usually do when they think it important to help others."

He patted her shoulder in paternal fashion and went back to Walter to inform him of his decision. Anne managed to sit there quietly until after Walter had escorted the judge to his car. Then the reaction came, and she hurried into her shop before she could disgrace herself. End of furor? Everything would be as it had been before Mona had talked her into displaying those statues out there?

Good heavens, the owner and operator of the Santa Fe Rise and Shine Company had been right when he'd said the morning would grow on her! Robert Lund or no Robert Lund, it was so a great morning in old Santa Fe, New Mexico!

Chapter Two

Around noon, the creator of the copper-foil monstrosities elected to favor the Indian Arts Shoppe with his presence and appetite. He smiled with a certain charm at Anne and a certain hope at Nora O'Dell. "If you have funds," he announced to Nora, "I'm willing to eat. They do a nice steak at La Fonda."

Nora declared heatedly, "You can chisel your steaks from somebody else."

"Is that sweet?" Tom Zimmerman asked. "Is it?"

Amused, Anne waved him to a chair. After checking the shop aisles, she waved Nora permission to go to lunch. Diminutive Nora left in a large hurry, her spike heels all but drilling into the wooden floor. Tom shoved his greasy blond hair out of his eyes and asked, "What was all that about?"

"Loretta Turley."

"Hmmmm."

Obviously buying time for thought, Tom took cigarette makings from his shirt pocket. He manufactured a Bull Durham cigarette with surprisingly deft movements of his chunky, blunt-ended fingers. After he'd twisted the paper at each end, he settled the cigarette in the righthand corner of his mouth and lighted up. The unfilled end of the cigarette flared up briefly, an event that left him undisturbed. After the fire had gone out, he drew smoke into his lungs and let it out slowly through his nose.

"I'd almost forgotten Loretta Turley's name," he finally said. "I'm doing a thing I call: *Greek Maiden With Urn*. In my thinking, that's always the name I apply to Loretta."

"The statue sounds almost conventional."

"It is. There Loretta stands in classical attire in a classical pose. It amuses me to think that long after Loretta has acquired the usual wrinkles and

18

sags, *Greek Maiden With Urn* will charm the world with her fresh beauty, her eternal spirit of spring."

Almost automatically, Anne ransacked her mind for the name of a likely buyer.

"But then again," Tom said, "I may smash the thing before I've completed it."

"Why?"

Anne's indignant brown eyes amused him. "You must work harder," he said, "to overcome your present instincts. My dear little moneygrubber, a creation is right or it isn't right. When they're right, they survive. When they're not right, they're destroyed."

"But suppose I offered you two hundred dollars right now for the statue as she stands?"

"I do my best thinking," Tom countered instantly, "while I'm eating a properly broiled steak."

Several women came into the shop. They studied the four long rows of well-filled display cases, the crowded wall racks, the Indian pottery piled on the floor. They deployed through the shop in the bustling manner of women who'd actually come to buy. Anne stayed put until a whitehaired woman exhibited a genuine interest in the *Maria* pieces on display in a locked wall cabinet. She hurried to the woman and unlocked the case. The woman, it developed, knew *Maria* pottery. She tipped a shallow bowl under a light to check the

19

quality of the polished black surfaces. Next, very carefully, she examined the dull black feather pattern that was characteristic of the work of Maria Martinez of the San Idlefonso Pueblo. Lastly, she looked at the underside of the bowl for the signature.

But fifty dollars!

Anne said easily, patiently, "All these pieces are authentic, ma'am. That's why I call this place the Indian Arts Shoppe. To me, to others, these things are superb examples of folk art. Naturally, they cost a bit more than strictly tourist stuff."

"And those horrors out in the patio?" the woman asked. She smiled a merry challenge. "What do you call those? Art?"

Near the desk, Tom Zimmerman coughed faintly.

"Be warned," Anne told the woman. "That's the sculptor trying to contain himself."

Interestingly, the woman went to the desk and sat on a corner of it. "When I saw those horrors," she said, "I wondered why the sculptor disliked women. Why do you, young man?"

Tom stood up. Tall, pathetically thin, downright shabby in levis and a denim shirt, he just ambled up front and went outdoors. The elderly woman smiled ruefully. "I suppose," she said, "that retreat was expressive of a point of view, too. But I was genuinely interested. As a matter of

20

fact, I think his work is brilliant. I just think it a pity that he fritters his talent away on trash like that."

Anne said tactfully, "Judge Langley resolved the issue this morning, ma'am. He denied the plea for an injunction forbidding me to display those statues."

"Oh, don't go on the defensive with me, young lady. When I said trash, I wasn't referring to so-called immorality. I call the things trash because Mr. Zimmerman's satire of certain unfortunate women is rather pedestrian. The concept doesn't do justice to his ability."

The other women came to the desk. One had several Indian dolls; the other had a Chimayo handbag. The woman who'd bought the dolls said a surprising thing to the elderly critic of Tom Zimmerman's work. "Nell," she said, "it was your idea that we buy something here to encourage this girl to fight the good fight for art."

Anne, startled, almost dropped one of the dolls.

"I'm Miss Aley," the elderly woman introduced herself. "We've all admired your courage, young lady. It isn't easy, is it, to fight for a principle?"

"Whoa," Anne told her. "To be frank, Miss Aley, I really wasn't fighting for a principle. Tom needed a place to show his things, and I like Tom

21

well enough to want to help him. That's the truth."

"Well, be that as it may. Do you know any other *avant-garde* artists?"

"If I don't, my roomie does. She's Mona Yates, art critic for the *Santa Fe Viewer*. We have the strangest house you'll ever see on Canyon Road. Once a week, on Sunday afternoon, in fact, we have the Santa Fe equivalent of a salon. Fellows and girls come to show their art or to talk art while I stuff them with enchiladas and frijoles and rice and coffee."

With seeming irrelevance, Miss Aley said crisply, "I think I'll have those two matched Maria bowls, Miss Hendlay. Aren't they exquisite? But then, all true art is exquisite. Are these salons open to the public, by the way?"

"Well, we won't throw uninvited guests out on their ears, Miss Aley. But they are pretty rough brawls, sometimes. They're much too much for me. I usually stay in the kitchen until there's no one left to feed."

"It sounds quite exciting," the elderly lady said. "You're a lucky girl, Miss Hendlay. You have youth, beauty, an obviously prosperous shop, and a most unusual social life. Isn't it a pity that not all women are as fortunate?"

The ladies were leaving when Tom Zimmerman

returned with a plastic-wrapped loaf of sheepherder's bread he'd bought in the Indian outdoor market under the portal of the Palace of Governors. Tom studiously avoided looking at Miss Aley. He grinned, though, when he'd made himself comfortable beside the desk. "In her girlish little way," he said mockingly, "the peasant climbs. It fascinates me to see you climb, incidentally. You do it with such zest."

To needle him, Anne used a crudity that always bruised the tender sensibilities of Mr. Tom Zimmerman. "You always talk baloney," she said, "after you've chickened under criticism. I wonder why."

Tom flushed. He opened the plastic wrap with strong pulls of animal-like teeth and tore off a chunk of bread. He ate greedily, with a somewhat pitiful compulsiveness. Anne did pity him, but she managed to keep pity out of her manner as well as her voice.

"Regardless of what anyone says about your work," she pep-talked, "you have to do it as your instincts tell you to do it. The work is you, the expression of your own talent, your own thinking, your own emotional reaction to your own observations. My goodness, why didn't you just laugh at Miss Aley? Why didn't you just tell her that you made those so-called horrors because the women who inspired them were horrors?"

"You're really quite ignorant," Tom asked, "aren't you?"

"Probably." Anne smiled, entirely unconcerned. "My trouble was that I never studied especially well if I disliked a subject. Back in Idaho, a teacher once predicted that no self-respecting farmer would have me for a wife because I was so uncaringly impractical. Well, she was right in the sense that I never did catch me a farmer. I refuse outright to learn the things a farmer's wife ought to know, so the farmers never paid much attention to me. But I do know a few things, too. I did learn typing and shorthand and a lot more about the secretarial art. And retailing. As secretary to the great Sol Blumberg, I did learn a great deal about retailing."

"Dear peasant, the ignorance I made reference to involves art, the world of art. The lady who called my statues horrors just happens to be the proprietor of an influential art gallery in San Francisco. Miss Aley even knows a few trifles about art."

Anne began to smile, but Tom's expression wasn't that a man just talking to hear himself talk. "Well," she finally laughed, "we get all kinds here. She and her friends made their purchases here to encourage me, they said, to make the good fight for art. I suppose I should've guessed they were somebody in the art world. You can't just casually

24

spend a hundred and fifty dollars if you're not a somebody."

"What else did she come here for?"

"What else?"

"She's been prowling around for several weeks, dear peasant. There's a rumor, entirely unconfirmed, that she's hunting for talented young things to exploit."

Nora came back from lunch. A little man with a large bald head followed her in and came directly to the desk. Tom chickened once more, and in his anxiety to get away forgot his sack of sheepherder's bread. Amused, Anne wagged a forefinger at the little man. "I won't have you in here any more, Mr. Curzon," she said. "when an artist's on the premises. You scare them."

"Young lady, I notice that the obscenities are still on display."

"The statues are, yes, sir. Judge Langley decided this morning, however, that they're not obscene. I think the announcement will be made in this afternoon's papers."

"How much did you pay him?"

It interested Anne that this man, this adult, was utterly unable to believe even for an instant that he could be wrong in his opinion of the statues. She didn't dignify the question with an answer.

"Well," he snapped, "maybe I shouldn't have asked that. Judge Langley has a good reputation.

25

We won't be happy, however, if the statues remain on display. In fact, the association I represent will be actively unhappy, Miss Hendlay. You know what that means, I presume."

"I'm afraid so," Anne admitted. "Having failed to get an injunction, having failed to persuade the district attorney to act against me, and having failed to arouse the people of Santa Fe, your association will now try to boycott me into a more cooperative frame of mind."

Mr. Curzon was indignant. "You make it sound," he charged, "as if we were unreasonable people trying to bully you."

"I think you are unreasonable," Anne told him mildly. "The only definition of art that you'll accept is your own definition. Yet you're not an artist. You know less about art than I, in fact, and I don't profess to know very much. I can't define art. Even dictionaries define it differently, and to define it they use other words they can't define precisely, either. But *you* know what art is! And you'll boycott anyone who doesn't agree with your definition."

Suddenly, almost startlingly, Mr. Curzon smiled. "Well, there's another solution possible," he said. "We could buy the statues, perhaps. You see, in our own way, we're trying to be good citizens. We do think the statues are obscene. We don't want them out there for children to giggle at, and we don't want decent women mocked as those statues mock them. Very well. We protested to the proper authorities, as was our right. We sought an injunction, as was our right. We've complained to you, as was our right. Now we offer to buy them, as is our right."

"And then you'll destroy them, sir?"

"Our disposition of them, Miss Hendlay, would be our affair. I'm at liberty to offer three hundred dollars for each statue. That would be fifteen hundred dollars. I can give you a check here and now, and I can have a truck call for them within an hour."

Nora, having heard, hustled outdoors and got Tom Zimmerman back into the shop. Tom gave little Mr. Curzon a walleyed look of fear that amused the man. "I never eat artists," he said promptly. "I don't even dislike artists, young man. I do wish, however, that talented men such as you would overcome the very bad modern habit of drawing your inspiration from the seamier aspects of life. Isn't the sweetness of a woman worthy of attention? Or the animalistic gayety of a child? Why must you people always sensationalize . . . or mock . . . or tear down?"

Anne said quickly, to avoid a long debate, "Mr. Curzon wants to buy all five statues, Tom, for fifteen hundred dollars. If you accept the offer, I'll waive my customary commission."

Tom reached for his sack of bread. He looked Mr. Curzon up and down. "Peasant," Tom said. Tom smiled, chucked Nora under the chin and again ambled to the door.

Chapter Three

Robert Lund was both astonished and baffled when Anne told him about the offer and its refusal. Not a man to talk and drive at the same time, however, Robert made no comments until after he'd pulled into a Shell station in Bernalillo and had told the attendant to fill the tank and check the water, oil and tires. "Incredible," Robert then said. He shook his head. "Only the very poor," he went on, "seem able to be that indifferent to money. Interesting."

"Of course," Anne explained, "Tom knew what Mr. Curzon intended to do with those statues. I can understand Tom's unwillingness to have them destroyed. Women those statues may be to those who look at them, but in a sense they're Tom's children."

Robert said indignantly, "But the fellow's a moocher! How much money has he mooched from you?"

"None."

"Oh, sure."

"Oh, I'm not saying that he doesn't put the bite on me for eating money from time to time. He does. Fred Vicks does. Peter does. And so on. But my old boss Sol Blumberg taught me in Denver to be meticulous about keeping records of the money I'm owed. So I keep records. Sooner or later I sell something for these artists. When that happens, I deduct from the loot received the money the artist owes me, plus my commission. A couple of months ago I sold a couple of pieces of patio statuary for Tom. Account squared."

"If you invested the money you lend these people in good growth stocks, you'd get dividends plus an increase of your capital."

"But I wouldn't be handling their work, would I? Someone else would come along to help them out with loans, and that person would get their things to handle."

The attendant came to the window to say that everything had been checked out, and Robert gave him his credit card. While the financial matters were being seen to, Anne swung around on the front seat of the Buick to check the picnic hamper and the filled water jugs in the rear. All was well. They'd not perish of thirst or starvation even if the car broke down somewhere on that vast, apparently empty land spread northwest of little Bernalillo. After she'd swung around and refastened her seat belt, she checked her wallet to make certain once again that she had everything a girl needed when she was foraging in Indian country for handicrafts to sell in her shop. Her serious, methodical manner amused Robert. "You can always write a check, you know," he reminded her. "The Indian isn't an untutored aborigine, if he ever was."

"Some like cash; others like traveler's checks; others take personal checks. And don't mock my way of doing business. As Sol Blumberg always told me, you can't go wrong if you satisfy your wholesalers and your customers."

They pushed off by way of State Highway 44 under a clear April sky and a mellow sun. Before them for as far as they could see lay Indian country, a spectacular land of mesas and lofty mountains, of colorful vistas and far horizons. West of Bernalillo, on a height overlooking the storied Rio Grande, they caught a glimpse of the Coronado State Monument. If one chose to swing off the highway, one could see with his own eyes the ruins of the Indian pueblo of Kuaua, where Coronado and his army were reputed to have spent the winter of 1540-41. But there was no time now for a girl and her fellow to roam through the fifteen-hundred-room pueblo as they'd done last year. Business had to be business, after all.

The road carried them to a country of rolling hills dotted with piñon and juniper. Robert, surprisingly, decided to drive and talk at the same time. And being Robert, he ended the fiction of being indifferent to the fact that the compromise he'd arranged hadn't been made.

"Right now," he said suddenly, "my family isn't happy with you. I make no complaints because you didn't even approach Mrs. Staunton after I'd made all the prelimiary arrangements. But my family does wonder why you didn't accept the opportunity to extricate yourself from that mess. It was a graceful way out."

"Walter Sward thought that the disposition of the statues was irrelevant."

Robert grimaced.

"Well, what was involved," Anne explained nervously, "was a matter of principle. I didn't quite understand everything that Walter said at the time, but I did begin to understand when Mr. Curzon visited the store on Thursday afternoon. He threatened me with a boycott. It never seemed to occur to him that he could be wrong. I was to

31

do what he wanted me to do, or else. Well, I do have my rights, don't I?"

"I'll have a chat with him," Robert promised grimly.

Anne loved the hardening of his jaws, the tightening of his chin muscles. All men, she thought, should be as ferociously eager to defend their women. Brown eyes softly aglow, she studied his face until a flush told her she was making him self-conscious. Tactfully, she gazed out the window at a distant mesa. The bluff was a delicate lavender and quite precipitous, but its flat, mile-long top had a golden sheen suggestive of water bowing on eternally under the eternal sun.

"What makes it difficult for me," Robert confided, "is that my mother and aunt think that you've been corrupted by these artists. You don't know it, but a couple of Sundays ago my mother and aunt decided to pay you an afternoon call. You were having a rowdy party, to hear them tell it. Some raggle-taggle bearded fellows and greasy-haired girls were caterwauling an anti-John Birch Society song in your patio. A girl in a Bikini was doing a grotesque Indian dance while the others sang."

Anne swallowed, imagining the scene without too much difficulty.

"Now it's all right for boys to be boys and girls to be girls," Robert said. "When I was at Stanford

University in California, I cut loose a few times myself. But men aren't boys and women aren't girls. And in any event, my mother and aunt expect a bit more of a potential Lund."

"I see."

"What bothers them most," Robert went on, "isn't that you have these so-called salons every Sunday afternoon, though they don't approve of them. No, what really bothers them is that these people are your friends. My aunt asked how come that people such as these are your only friends in Santa Fe."

"But that's not ture! There's Walter Sward. There are my friends in the business community. Why, I even have friends among the Indians."

"Anyway, Anne, it would've helped a lot had you accepted the compromise. By keeping those things on display, you're confirming my family's belief that you're no better, really, than all those —well, hippies."

They passed through Cuba, and now the road left the mountains behind to span high plateau country. In the distance, earth and sky seemed to blend on the horizon. Not anywhere in that vast land did anything move. Anne was convinced that if the car were stopped and their breaths held, she'd hear not a sound—not even the vibrations of all those lovely colors.

"Could you end the salons?" Robert asked.

33

Anne gave it the serious thought due the problem. Deep within her an odd warmth stirred. Peculiarly, her toes tingled in her crepe-soled, denim-topped casuals. It came to her that some time between Thursday morning and this moment, Robert Lund had made a decision concerning their futures. The cracks of Mona, Walter, Tom, Fred, Peter and others notwithstanding, Robert wasn't the sort of man who went his rich, stuffy, traditionalist way without concern for the right of other people to lead their lives as they wanted to.

"I have nerve asking that," Robert conceded gruffly. "I can't say, for example, that if you'll be more conventional I'll place an engagement ring on your finger. But it might help to make that possible in the end."

Anne said, thinking she owed it to her integrity, "Yours is a very strange family, Robert, my bucko."

"It's all a matter of perspective, I suppose. I read somewhere, I think in Durrell, that the world changes remarkably when you look at it from different positions. Look at it; then take two paces east or west and look at it again. A different world each time."

Anne found the words she was groping for in all that delicious warmth and tingling stirring through her. "When I told my mother about you," she said simply, "all my mother said is that she hoped we'd be happy. She never asked what you do, who your friends are, how you live."

Robert nodded. Anne saw wistfulness come and go in his somber hazel eyes.

"I'll have to think about it," Anne told him presently. "The salons are fun, and I like fun. And they serve a business purpose, too. You can't really get art out of people if they're always hungry. Not that I feed that army only for commercial reasons, understand. I love to cook. I love to see people chomping away happily at table. But it is a fact that some of those folks can use a square meal at least once a week."

"But if you were a mother, Anne, and you had eight million dollars to pass along to your son one day, wouldn't you be concerned that he should marry the right girl?"

When she could speak, Anne said huskily, "That's a heap of money."

"A heap of social responsibility."

They reached Blanco Trading Post, and they parked off the road to eat their lunch. A scraggly dog came along, waving its tail for a hand-out, and Robert fed it pieces of chicken stripped off the bone. Anne wished as she looked at man and dog that she'd remembered to bring her camera. For some reason, he looked infinitely more relaxed and boyish than she'd ever seen him. The possibility that she was the reason, or at least the decision he'd made concerning their futures, did occur to her, and the thought increased the pleasure she got out of just looking at him while he fed the dog and occasionally scratched its back. But there were other thoughts, too, less pleasing ones because they suggested there were far too many tough problems to solve. How could she marry this man, for example, rather than a family? How could she marry this individual, for example, rather than history or a financial institution? How could she have in marriage the personal life any adult wanted to enjoy? Or to put it differently: how could she have her own friends and her own interests despite family objections to both? Certainly those questions would have to be answered at least partially to her own satisfaction before she became other than just a date to him. Give up Mona, her friends, her business? The family, if not the man, asked a lot.

"I was thinking," Robert said, interrupting her thoughts, "about the first time I met you. It wasn't an auspicious beginning. I've never liked to see women in slacks, and you were in slacks. I've never liked brisk women, and you were brisk."

"You came at a bad time," Anne insisted, laughing. "I'd just moved into the Indian Arts Shoppe. I had very little money, so I had to do my own work. In you came just after I'd spread some tile goop on the bathroom wall. I could have cheerfully clouted you!"

Her lovely face, a smoother golden tan dominated by merrily flashing brown eyes, inspired him to blow a kiss at her. But he said seriously, always serious about business or money matters, "I wish I'd known you before you invaded Santa Fe to open that shop. I could have made it easier for you."

"Oh, I was never in danger of starving, Robert. My old boss told me that if things didn't work out, he'd give me a job again in Denver. And my parents were sweet about fending cash gifts from time to time."

"But it all worked out, didn't it? I've often wondered why. I mean, Santa Fe is loaded with shops that sell Indian things to tourists. Your shop off Cortez Alley doesn't have the best location for the tourist trade. Yet you're quite successful."

"Luck. Some planning and retailing knowhow, yes, but most luck."

"Could you close tomorrow, do you think?"

Ann's first reaction was pain, definite pain. Then, shocked, she asked: "Why ever would I do that?"

"I could find a proper job for you," Robert said. "We could move you into a proper environment, too. My mother and aunt would see to it that you bought the right clothes, met the right people, were invited to join the right clubs, were included in the right social affairs."

Anne said—she couldn't help it—"You ask a lot, Robert."

"Some would say that I'm offering a lot."

Troubled, Anne began to gather the picnic gear.

"You might think about it," Robert suggested. "The truth is that I'm in a difficult position. I am a Lund, I do have obligations to my family, and I do have social responsibilities I have to meet. If I could be more flexible, there'd be no delays, no conditions. But that's how it is, I'm afraid."

Anne did think about it, her emotions mixed, and the fun of the buying trip ended there. She was indifferent to the countryside until they reached Shiprock. After they'd each gotten a room in the motel owned and operated by the Navajo tribe, she did come aware enough to go into the town proper to purchase various cases of top-quality Navajo jewelry. But after that, dinner with Robert was disturbing, the night was sleepless, and the long drive back to Santa Fe on Sunday a downright bore.

Why in the world, she wondered, did she have to prove she was *worthy* of him?

Chapter Four

Mrs. Elmo Staunton was annoyed. "In fact," she elaborated in the Indian Arts Shoppe on Tuesday afternoon, "I'm seriously annoyed with you, Anne Hendlay."

Mystified, Anne invited the woman to have tea with her at her desk. Up front, Nora O'Dell was having a ball selling some of the new Navaho jewelry to a couple of hearty, genial men with the good cheer of Texas in their voices. The men were arguing that the jewelry couldn't be good because the asking price was so low. Nora was happily engaged in the unusual task of trying to justify low prices instead of high prices. The technique Nora was using was interesting, and Anne wished to hear every word of it. Still, Mrs. Staunton was Mrs. Staunton.

"I don't feel hurt," Mrs. Staunton said, "by

your odd refusal to invite me to your Sunday afternoon salon. While I wish I could attend, I do appreciate that I'm several years older than the artists and models who attend. But is Nell Aley my junior? I'm insulted!"

"I'm not guilty," Anne said composedly. She poured the Japanese green. "Miss Aley was there when I got home from Shiprock, Mrs. Staunton. Apparently no one had invited her. According to Mona, Miss Aley arrived at around four o'clock, said, 'How nice!' and just proceeded to make herself at home."

"I expect an invitation this Sunday."

At sixty, straight as a fence post, forceful as a gamecock, Mrs. Staunton looked Anne dead in the eye—formidable, even frightening in her determination not to be outdone by Miss Nell Aley.

Anne asked soothingly, "Would you really do me the honor, Mrs. Staunton? We'll probably seem terribly gauche and silly—which is the reason I've not asked you before."

Mrs. Staunton was mollified. "One expects the young to be gauche," she said generously. "Perhaps gaucherie is one of the charms of the young. Very well. Now that I understand the circumstances under which Miss Aley attended last Sunday, I'll think no more about the matter. Now then, what will you charge our Plateau Club for an hour lecture this Thursday afternoon on your experiences as a buyer and seller of Indian art objects?"

Anne laughed. "Glory," she said, "I never give talks."

"We could probably scrounge a hundred dollars together," Mrs. Staunton said.

Anne said promptly, "I give talks. They may be informal, I may garble syntax, but I give talks."

"You see," Mrs. Staunton said as one knowledgeable woman to another, "Rome was not built in a day. The unknown must make herself known. With charm, with tact, with undiscernible skill, she must make her way into her proper social milieu. Impeccable sponsors do help initially—indeed, they're requisite to social success. But in any social mielieu, one eventually must make her way on her own."

All of which was about as comprehensible to Anne as any Indian language.

"Oh," Mrs. Staunton said excitedly, "I do hear little secrets from time to time. While I disagree entirely with dear Mrs. Lund and Miss Symonds that you must be groomed, so to speak, I'm perfectly willing to donate my time to this cause."

Now Anne began to understand a bit too much. "I didn't know," she said, "that I'd reached the grooming stage."

Nora O'Dell came back with a seventy-five-dollar personal check for Anne to okay for accep-

41

tance. Anne smiled at the men, nodded to Nora. After the redhead had gone up front again, Mrs. Staunton smiled. "I imagine you'll miss this little shop, Anne, won't you? It's a nice little business. I've always been most impressed by the cheery service and the cleanliness."

Anne decided that perhaps she ought to slow the tempo a bit. She said with typical candor, "I'm not engaged to Robert, Mrs. Staunton. We've reached no understanding of any kind."

"Indeed?"

But other customers came in, what seemed to be a busload of tourists with little time in which to do considerable shopping. Anne had to go up front to help out. It was a good half-hour before all the men and women could be attended to, and of course Mrs. Staunton left long before Anne returned to her desk.

Nora counted the loot. "Not a fortune, Miss Hendlay," she called from the register; "just a nice two hundred and ninety dollars so far."

"What did that last flurry bring in?"

"About eighty dollars." Nora closed the cash-register drawer, looking puzzled. "How come, Miss Hendlay," she asked, "that the bus stopped here? Usually the tours go over to the Plaza."

"Whose bus was it?"

"Bullet Mike's."

Anne got the telephone number from the directory and promptly dialed Bullet Mike's office. She was eventually connected with a bass-voiced man who said, "Bullet here—shoot."

Anne's perfectly natural question delighted him. "Miss Hendlay," he said, "you must be a bright kid. You'd be surprised if you knew how many dumb jerks there are doing business in Santa Fe. Wouldn't you think more people would know enough to call a guy and at least thank him for taking a bundle of dough to their shops?"

"Do I thank you with a weekly check, or cash, or what, Mr.—er—do I call you Bullet?"

"Why not? I'm not proud! Now I'm glad you spoke about dough, Miss Hendlay. I opened this office about four months ago. What I'm trying to do, natch, is take my clients to places where the other tours don't take them. Sure, I show them the regular sights. I have to do that. But I also advertise I show them a lot of Sante Fe the average tour doesn't show them. Like the Indian Arts Shoppe, maybe, if we could make a little arrangement."

"Ten percent of the gross sales, Bullet?"

"What about fifty bucks a week?"

"How many busloads a week would you bring me?"

"Three a day."

Anne had to laugh. "Now you're giving me a problem, Bullet," she reported. "To be fair or not to be fair! Well, I'll be fair. You'll make more money if you take the deal I proposed. For instance, eight dollars would be due you right now under that arrangement."

"Hey!"

"Take the ten percent," Anne advised. "I'm not being silly, either. The more money you make, the happier you'll be with the arrangement. Which means that I'll make more money, too."

"The other way, though, I'll know what I can expect each week."

"I see. Well, it's up to you, Bullet. I'll mail a check on Saturday. All right?"

"It's a deal, Miss Hendlay. I think you're being smart. I wish others weren't the dumb jerks they are. There's a lot of loot in tourists if you show them a good time and give them value for their dough."

When Anne hung up, Nora poured tea for herself and sat where Mrs. Staunton had sat. The diminutive redhead said a bit embarrassedly, "I have rabbit ears, Miss Hendlay. I heard just enough of your conversation with Mrs. Staunton to catch the drift. If you ask me, I think the ladies of the Plateau Club will give you a rough time. Maybe they didn't side officially with Mr. Curzon's association, but they gave the association a lot of support. I can tell you why they did, too."

"So?"

"What's happening in Santa Fe right now," Nora said, "is very interesting. Mrs. Staunton is really gone on art, and she's got a lot of the rich women steamed up about making Santa Fe the art capital of the west. Loretta heard a couple of the women talking things over. Loretta was posing for that Mrs. Quinn who thinks she's an artist. I guess it never occurred to the women that Loretta wasn't deaf."

"Sounds conspiratorial," Anne teased.

"Well, in a way, maybe it was. The women figured out that year in and year out, their social group is the best steady market the artists have. So then they figured out they're strong enough to shape the kind of art they want to see develop in Santa Fe. One woman said that if they'd been properly organized before you showed the statues, they could have forced Tom Zimmerman not to make them, let alone show them."

Anne stopped smiling. "But that's dictatorship!" she protested.

Nora said unhappily, "I've been noticing something, Miss Hendlay, ever since the statues went on display and they kicked up all that fuss. A lot of the Plateau Club women have stopped buying from us. I know that we've been taking in more money, a lot more money, but that's because the fuss attracted tourists to us."

"Really?"

45

"If you ask me, Miss Hendlay, I think that what Mrs. Staunton is doing is luring you to a meeting so that the members can ask you a lot of questions about your attitude and things like that. Everybody knows that you're in with the younger artists. If they could make a deal with you, they'd be that much ahead. If they couldn't make a deal with you—well, at least they'd know where they stand."

"When may I talk with Loretta?"

Nora giggled. "Nobody knows, I guess, Loretta least of all. That girl! She's dangling three fellows on three different strings—and is she ever busy!"

"Try to arrange it, Nora, will you? Oh, and you may as well write Mrs. Staunton a little note to the effect that I've changed my mind about speaking to the ladies. And, of course, withdraw my invitation to attend the salon this Sunday. Just say, very delicately, that I think she's a snake-in-the-grass."

"Why can't I just say it bluntly?" Nora asked reasonably. "Once they get the artists under control, they can control the prices."

"Nope. I was raised by civilized people, you see. Be civilized at all times, there's the ticket!"

But disturbed, if civilized, Anne paid one of her rare visits to Mona's cubbyhole office at the headquarters of the *Santa Fe Viewer*. She caught lovely Mona wearing a green eyeshade and a grubby smock, and Mona didn't thank her for that. "It better be good, darling," Mona snapped. "I abhor people who interrupt me while I'm doing my Sunday feature."

Anne passed the news along to her. Quite interested, Mona listened without interruption. "Just fine," she said when Anne had finished. "I've heard some rumors that substantiate Loretta's tale. As a matter of fact, Miss Aley alluded to the subject at the salon last sunday. Interesting. But I really don't think that money's involved. That crowd has always dealt generously with Santa Fe artists. Really! I'm inclined to think that the objective would be power. You know Mrs. Staunton. She fancies herself an authority on art. I think she'd find it agreeable to be the big cheese."

Anne said, outraged: "Paint what I tell you to paint—or starve. I don't buy that, Mona."

Mona nodded, obviously not buying it, either. She said quite practically, however: "It would be easier and more rewarding for you personally, Anne, to qualify for marriage to Robert Lund. The man is handsome, quite kind according to his lights, and he does have all that lovely money."

"And that outrages me, too, to be frank. I may not be rich or high society, but I'm a human being. You marry a human being not all the rest."

"The point I'm trying to make, darling, is that the mother and the aunt are part of that crowd. Their image of you wouldn't be improved if you

47

battled the Plateau Club tooth and nail—as I suspect you're thinking of doing."

Anne said emotionally, "Darned right! Look what they tried to do with Tom's statues. They were wrong, entirely wrong, according to a judge. Well, give them control of art in Santa Fe and then imagine what they'd do!"

Mona's blue eyes twinkled. "I don't know why," Mona said softly, "but I have a notion that here beginneth a lovely brawl. How nice! I was afraid it might be a dull summer.' "

Chapter Five

In the hope of strengthening her financial position before the "lovely brawl" began, Anne Hendlay wrote still another letter to Mr. Solomon Blumberg in Denver. She argued that if Indian handicrafts could be sold profitably in Santa Fe, New Mexico, they could be sold just as profitably in each of the cities in the five states where the

Blumberg Variety Store sign hung over the sidewalks. She then argued that she was the ideal person to function as his buyer, on a commission basis, in the Indian country adjacent to Santa Fe. "After all, sir," she wrote, "I know your retailing system thoroughly, I know Indian handicrafts, and I have broad contacts out in the country where the things are made." She sent the letter to Denver via special delivery. . . .

In Denver the following morning, after she'd read the letter, Mr. Blumberg's mail secretary said, "Tsk, tsk, tsk." Why won't people who profess to know our setup," she asked, "ever address their mail to the right person?" The letter was routed to the general manager's suite and was eventually placed in the "In" tray on the desk of the acquisitions supervisor. When the mail was brought in, Mr. Ewing commented bitterly, "People write too many letters these days. Every time you look around, you see someone bring mail in."

Mr. Ewing wasn't a man who read his mail until it was a question of either reading it or ordering another "in" basket to take care of the overflow. He didn't get around to Anne's letter until several mornings later, when his secretary said, "My goodness, sir, there's an envelope with a special delivery stamp!" Mr. Ewing scowled. "If it was so important," he asked, "why didn't the guy

49

telephone?" But, dutifully, he took the letter from the opened envelope and read it.

"Well, well, well," Mr. Ewing chuckled. "I always loved this little lady. No matter what Mr. Blumberg roared, she'd always get you in to see him if you had to see him. She is a real sweet kid."

"Who's that, sir?"

"Before your time. Anne Hendlay. She was Mr. Blumberg's secretary when this was just a three-state retailing complex. She was always begging the man to let her train to manage a store. But Mr. Blumberg's policy then was what it is now. So one day she quit to open a store of her own down in Santa Fe."

"I think it's a shame," the secretary protested, "that women have so little opportunity here."

"So it's a shame," Mr. Ewing agreed. "So what?"

Mr. Ewing gave thought to the letter during lunch in the company dining room. The more he thought about this newest version of Anne Hendlay's old proposition, the better he liked it. Buyers who knew their stuff usually wanted umpteen dollars a year on a million-year contract that bound the company but left them free to make a better deal elsewhere whenever they liked. Another reason Mr. Ewing liked the deal was that the company, in his opinion, could use a new line advantageously. Indian stuff would be relatively new

50

on the retailing level at which the company operated. The relatively new line would give them an edge on the competition, for even if the junk didn't move, it would attract novelty seekers into the stores. Any time you could attract a ton of people into a store, Mr. Ewing thought, you were money ahead. Regardless of the twaddle women uttered about being shrewd shoppers, most women were impulsive buyers. Once they were in a store, most women bought. Okay. So women attracted by a new line in all two hundred and thirty Blumberg Variety Stores would buy something in all two hundred and thirty places. Would that be bad, especially when your buyer knew her stuff, knew your clientele, and was willing to work for five percent of the pennies the company was willing to spend for Indian junk? Suppose the company were willing to invest a hundred thousand? The buyer would cost a measly five thousand. Yet the advertising value derived ultimately from her work, her purchases, would be worth, at the very least, a couple of hundred thousand.

Mr. Ewing liked the results of his analysis. He glanced around the dining room and finally spotted the advertising manager having lunch with the sales manager. Mr. Ewing invited himself to join them for coffee and cigars. "Men," he said genially, "could we or couldn't we use a new line?"

"Right now," the advertising manager declared

51

promptly, "I could use a new line to exploit more than I can use aspirin—and I have a headache."

Mr. Ewing tossed the letter onto the table. The men read. The sales manager chuckled. "Spunky little fish," he said admiringly. "Back in the old days, she was always asking me questions about sales techniques. That's a nice shop she's developed, by the way. I saw it last year while I was heading for Arizona. Nothing gaudy, you understand; nothing big. She probably nets only fifteen thousand a year for about an eighty-hour week."

"I could do things with Indians," the advertising manager said dreamily. "Offbeat copy with punch in every line."

The sales manager nodded to Mr. Ewing. "We'll back you up," he said. "And this is a good time to bring in a new line. It's definitely decided that we'll expand into Wyoming this summer. Mr. Blumberg's even picked the man to head the project. David Congdon. Hot shot manager of that money-maker in Salt Lake City."

For Mr. Ewing, that was quite enough. He returned to his office and dictated a longish memo detailing his reasons for urging acceptance of the proposition made in Anne Hendlay's letter. Stapled together, the memo and the letter were routed back to Mr. Blumberg's office. The mail secretary remembered the distinctive envelope. She read the memo unashamedly. "So there you are," she told her typist. "It always pays to go through proper channels." At two o'clock, Anne Hendlay's letter was finally delivered to Mr. Solomon Blumberg at his desk.

Tall, muscular, vigorous, Sol Blumberg read the memo first and then the letter. He boomed, "This girl should have been a man. If she'd been a man, I'd have made her a manager. But you women! You have this marriage monkey riding your backs. Just when you've trained a woman to be useful, she quits to marry and have children."

Sol gave the proposition deep thought. He agreed with Ewing and the others that a new line would be useful just now. He agreed also that it would be convenient to hire a buyer—if he wanted to hire a new buyer—who was entirely familiar with organizational methods and policies. But a woman! Worse, an attractive young woman who'd once sat in this very office and told him she had every intention of marrying and raising children the moment she was given the privilege of doing so. The probability was that just when she's become an asset to the firm she'd go off and marry.

Mrs. Myersen came in and asked, as was her job, "Have you made any decision yet, sir, concerning Mr. David Congdon? Our analysis group's returned from Wyoming with a batch of figures related to sites for the proposed new stores.

They're ready to answer questions and make recommendations, but there's no one around to ask the questions."

"It has to be David Congdon up there, Mrs. Myersen. The young fellow may be a nut, but he knows how to develop and manage a store."

"But if he won't return from Santa Fe, sir . . .?"

"Well, maybe I'll put Anne Hendlay on that problem. She owes me something, you know."

Well informed, as any competent executive secretary ought to be, Mrs. Myersen smiled. "I'm so pleased," she said, "that you've decided to make Anne a buyer down there. Anne was always so good to people here. Her job never went to her head. That's very remarkable, when you remember that she was probably the youngest executive secretary in Denver."

Sol laughed reminiscently. "The odd thing about that," he told her, "was that it was all accidental. Her predecessor left me high and dry, just like that, without notice—to be married, of course. I poked Anne into the slot until I could find a properly qualified woman. I was lucky. Having been my mail secretary, she'd developed an encyclopedic knowledge of our operations. Being young and ambitious, she was willing to work until all hours—and to learn. So I never did get around to replacing her until she got that bee in her bonnet that she wanted to be a retailer, not a secretary, until she married."

"Sir, if I may say so, I think she deserves a chance. Knowing Anne, I'm sure she knows how to buy Indian things."

Sol Blumberg nodded absently and told her to get hold of Anne Hendlay in Santa Fe. Anne sounded tired when she answered the telephone, and Sol Blumberg said promptly, "Now you know it's no sinecure to be a boss, Anne. How's business?"

"Mr. Blumberg! Such an honor! How's Mrs. Blumberg? How's Debbie? Tell Debbie we have a room in our house she can have for the summer."

"Okay, okay. You'll probably corrupt her with those Bohemian friends of yours, but Debbie said that last summer was a gasser, whatever a gasser is, and she's been hoping you'd have her again this summer."

"I'll write her an invitation tomorrow, sir. Not today. Today we did a record business, and I'm tired. I was just getting ready to close up and go bumming around the Indian reservations for the rest of the afternoon."

He scored her A for the subtle way she'd swung the conversation around to Indians. It was interesting, he mused, that a farm girl had managed to learn so much about good business methods. Or had she ever really had to learn? She had a talent for business, probably.

"I'm calling about something else," Sol Blumberg fenced. "There's a nut named David Congdon down there who should be up here. I was planning to put him in charge of an expansion into Wyoming. But the nut resigned in a letter that said he wanted, and I quote, to savor the romance of life in old Santa Fe in enchanted New Mexico. I stop quoting. If I didn't need the nut, I'd let him starve on all that romance. But I do need him, so you find him for me and get him back up here where he belongs."

"Is that the David Congdon who ran the store in Kanab, Utah?"

"I shoved him up to Salt Lake City just after you left. He's been my top manager in Utah."

"Any idea where the body is, sir?"

"No."

A singing quality came into her contralto voice as she said, "Well, no matter—Santa Fe's not an enormous city, you know."

Sol Blumberg loved those cheery, singing tones. If the girl had grown older, she still responded to challenge with all the zest of a colt.

"Nice of you," he said with the coolness he always used to conceal emotion. "Now about your proposition. We'll give you a five-thousand credit to pick up some Indian junk for market-testing purposes. Get a broad variety of things to retail for not more than ten dollars on a forty percent markup. If you want your five percent commission in advance, write Myersen. Okay?"

She said weakly, after a long, long time: "Thanks for the chance, Mr. Blumberg. If I can do so, I'll mail Mr. David Congdon back to you via special delivery."

Laughing, Sol Blumberg hung up.

Chapter Six

A tired but elated Anne Hendlay did close her shop after the telephone conversation with Sol Blumberg, and she did drive north with the idea of popping into the San Juan Pueblo to see what some of her Indian friends might have for sale on a percentage basis. Before she got out of Santa Fe, however, she decided that she'd done quite enough business for one day. She swung east and eventually worked her way to the pueblo-style house she shared with Mona on Canyon Road. Fred Vicks came out of his metal-crafts studio to supervise the tricky maneuvers necessary to back her car into the garage from the narrow street. Looking somewhat like a red-haired gorilla, with his bare torso and his long arms dangling at his sides, Fred closed the overhead door for her and then followed her into the patio.

"There's nothing like being rich," Fred said. "Only the rich can take an afternoon off."

Anne went on into the house und changed into shorts, a blouse and sandals. She got a tall bottle of Coca-Cola from the refrigerator and two glasses from the cupboard. Fred opened the bottle with his teeth, as he always did, but meticulously wiped the bottle top with his handkerchief before he poured. He exhaled with every indication of pleasure after he'd emptied half his glass with one prodigious swallow. "I could sure learn to love being rich," he anounced.

But Fred had come over with more important things to say. He pulled a crumpled newspaper clipping from his pocket and gave it to Anne to read. After she'd read it, he said worriedly, "A lot of those women are good customers. What happens if they open that Art Arcade they're talking about and say I have to sell all my stuff through them?"

58

Since Anne hadn't seen the story before, she had to think about the matter. There was no doubt in her mind that the Plateau Club was behind this hint by Mrs. Elmo Staunton and her associates of an Art Arcade to come. All the associates were members of the Plateau Club. All were women who'd stopped patronizing the Indian Arts Shoppe after Tom's statues had kicked up the art-versus-obscenity furor. Also, several of the women had telephoned her to scold her for refusing to come to the meeting of the Plateau Club to hear their views on the subject of art.

"What scares me," Fred reported, "is that if I market through just one place, I'll lose money."

"And if you don't market through them exclusively, you might lose those good customers?"

"Yup."

An artist's position in twentieth-century America was really rough, Anne decided. He was at the mercy of everyone, unless he was lucky enough to hit it big. If he didn't sell, he didn't eat; so when he took his things to galleries or even places like hers, he was really coming to the door with his hat in his hand. Usually he had to accept just about any proposition that was offered to him. That being the case, it was no accident that there were few wealthy artists in America.

"I was talking to Tom Zimmerman," Fred said thoughtfully. "Tom's thinking that all the fuss about his gals wasn't what it appeared to be. He says that Nora told him that—"

"Nora shouldn't talk so much," Anne interrupted. "And you shouldn't worry so much, it seems to me, until there's something to worry about. Talk about building an Art Arcade is just talk. The sort of thing mentioned in this article can't be created overnight even if someone were willing to put up the money. And there's another point. Most people with money don't invest that kind of money in any business until they're sure of a profit."

"But suppose they get a lot of artists signed up to market through them?"

The telephone rang in the house before Anne could answer. A pleasant but somewhat metallic voice informed her that Miss Nell Aley was speaking, and then Miss Aley invited Anne to her apartment for coffee, pastry and a chat. "I think you'll find the chat interesting," Miss Aley said. "In a sense, we're in the same business."

"Ma'am," Anne told her, I'm bushed. Between nine o'clock this morning and one o'clock this afternoon, my shop took in over five hundred dollars. A record! But I wore my legs out, and so did Nora."

"Could I come to you, then? It's important to our business interests, I'm afraid."

Anne asked, on a hunch: "The proposed Art Arcade?"

"Well, it does concern that in a limited way."

Anne invited her over. She told Fred to go back to work for a while, and she got coffee ready and made some finger sandwiches to go with the coffee. Miss Aley came alone in a taxi. She'd brought pastry with her. She approved the living room with eyes that didn't neglect to estimate the cash value of certain Indian art objects on the mantel shelf. "I've never been a devotee of folk art," she said, "and I suspect now that I've been missing some pleasurable moments."

Anne said ruefully, "I've learned to contain my enthusiasm for Indian art, Miss Aley, while I'm in these parts. I happen to think that the only genuine art extant is folk art. The expression is natural. Once you get into the formal arts, everything's so studied, worked over, contrived. But if I dare say that at one of our salons, I'm clobbered."

"As you ought to be, of course. A painting by Goya isn't less a work of art because it's an expression of the intellect as well as of emotion."

"I've been told that before." Anne laughed. "Oh, I've been told that before."

"Well, I'm not saying it now merely to rebut you, Miss Hendlay. It seems to me there's no room for dogmatism of any kind in the arts world. To do acceptable work, an artist must express himself truly. And that gets us to this Art Arcade thing you mentioned. What you're about to get here,

61

Miss Hendlay, is an attempt to impose a kind of dogma upon your local artists. This worries me. I get many fine things from Santa Fe for display and sale in San Francisco. But how long will I continue to get anything of value if your local artists are compelled to meet the dictates of a group capable of exercising full control over their methods and even their choice of subjects?"

"It would be rough," Anne agreed, "if the group did what you're afraid it would do."

Miss Aley asked softly, after some hesitation: "Are you vulnerable to reprisals, Miss Hendlay, if you resist this group in their attempt to take over?"

Anne was amused. "Glory, Miss Aley, I doubt I could get around to resisting any group effectively. My specialty is Indian arts. Oh, I handle a few things for some of the younger artists on a consignment basis, but that's just something I do for people I like. You mustn't get the idea that my little battle for Tom's statues stemmed from any genuine interest in what I call the formal arts."

"No ambitions to expand, in other words?"

"Well, not into that area, certainly. I've always been a nut about Indian arts. As soon as I could, I opened this business. Now I'm about to expand. By that I mean that I've become a local buyer of Indian stuff for a variety-store chain."

"If you'll forgive me," Miss Aley said, "you're a foolish young lady."

Anne chuckled amiably and served the coffee and finger sandwiches. Miss Aley ate quietly, her soft white face unreadable. She presently explained, "You're foolish, you see, because you're absolutely blind to an excellent business opportunity that's waiting for you to grab it. If I were your age, I'd open a shop here this very day to exploit that opportunity to the full."

Anne's business instincts were aroused. "You've lost me," she said simply.

"I attended the salon, young lady, pushed my way in uninvited, no less, to learn a few things about you. I learned what I wanted to learn. This place has become a kind of hangout for many of the most talented young artists in this region. You're liked by these people. You're a friend, in other words. Well, my dear girl, if I had that relationship with several hundred eager and sincere artists, I'd have an Arts Shoppe, not an Indian Arts Shoppe. Publicity on a regular basis—and Miss Mona Yates is your friend, isn't she, *and* the art critic of the *Santa Fe Viewer*. I'd have regular shows. I'd quicken an interest of people around here in forwarding the careers of young artists. And having done all this, I'd put substantial sums of money into the bank each week."

The weakness of the plan struck Anne at once.

"But you see," she remonstrated, "I know nothing about the formal arts."

Miss Aley smiled faintly. "I knew nothing, either," she admitted, "When I opened my first gallery. What you do, quite frankly, is get an advisory group together. In this case it would be relatively simple. Young people, especially artists, are always very willing to sit in judgment on the work of others. Make the venture a type of co-operative venture. Have regular days for judging, price-fixing, all that."

Anne was intrigued. "That could be fun," she conceded. "The way I cook for that army, they should give me their advice for free."

"That empty shop adjacent to yours could house the gallery," Miss Aley said. "Your only overhead would be the rent and publicity, because I'm sure that you and your assistant could find the time to make sales and such."

Now the pudgy white face of Miss Aley was readable.

Anne asked softly, "You'll pay the rent if I pay for the publicity and handle sales, Miss Aley?"

"Yes. I plan to close my gallery next year. I'm not as vigorous as I used to be. I like this city, the climate. I'll want something to do in my retirement, however—something that won't take up too much of my time. If you wanted to drop out for any reason—marriage, say—we could have the place appraised, and I'd buy you out."

Anne said mechanically, "I'll have to think it over, of course. Needless to say, you've taken me by surprise."

"I usually do surprise people," Miss Aley said contentedly. "I think that's why I'm a successful art dealer."

Several minutes later Miss Aley went out to her waiting cab, leaving Anne deep in thought behind her . . . a businesswoman tempted by opportunity . . . a girl scared stiff that she might be on the verge of making a catastrophic goof.

It was the fear of making a catastrophic goof that caused her to telephone Robert to come over for a home-cooked dinner. "Mona's lecturing at a high school," she announced, "on the Validity of Art even in a Pragmatic Society. Come early, and stay until she stumbles in!"

"What's the problem?"

"Problem?"

"You always sound terribly girlish and gay when you have a problem. Don't tell me that Tom wants to stand a nude in the Indian Arts Shoppe patio!"

"I'm afraid this could be an even bigger problem, Robert. I do need business advice."

Being Robert, he drove up less than an hour later, catching Anne still in shorts, blouse and

65

sandals. "We'll settle the problem," he said authoritatively, "and then I'll take you to dinner. Begin from the beginning, please."

He was less authoritative after she'd begun from the beginning and raced on through the middle to the end.

"How do you get into these things?" he asked. "And what ever happened to my idea that you close the shop and all that?"

Anne forced herself to say calmly, "I resented the idea, Robert, that I should prove myself worthy of marrying you. Here I am, as I am. That's all any girl can say, and that's all she can be, really. I'm not a low character. Meeting the right people or joining the right clubs won't make me a better character."

"That's not the point, you know. These are my family's wishes. It costs very little to humor them."

"Little? All my friends around here, the business I've developed? Those aren't little."

"So the answer to the main problem is to plunge deeper into the sort of life my family can't approve? Instead of one business, you'll have two businesses. Instead of extricating yourself from these idiotic people, you'll become closer to them than ever?"

Anne said hotly, "I'll marry you this afternoon, right now! I'll close my business before we leave

66

on a honeymoon! There's my real answer to the real problem!"

"I've told you I can't be flexible, Anne. If I must put it crassly, my mother and aunt control the money. Furthermore, I do happen to love them, respect them, want to please them."

"All I have, Robert," Anne said tautly, "means something to me, too. Asking me to throw away everything on the possibility I may please your family—well, that's just asking too much."

He blanched, did Robert Lund. Next he was on his feet, his face pinched, his eyes stubborn. He said softly, with a great display of good manners and restraint: "You asked me to advise you on a business matter. My advice is that if you're interested in business growth, you'd be foolish not to accept Miss Aley's offer. If you're at all interested in pleasing me and my family, on the other hand, then I advise you to follow my other suggestion. Do you mind if we don't go to dinner?"

He went to the patio gate. Anne waited, stricken, for him to turn around like a sensible man to work something out. But Robert Lund never did turn around. Instead, he got into his car and drove off.

Chapter Seven

The following afternoon Miss Aley came to the patio of the Indian Arts Shoppe with an easy rolling gait, her eyes squinted against the sun. Anne smiled at her politely but had to make an effort to sound at all interested in the business deal Miss Aley had proposed. For the first time in several years, business seemed so utterly unimportant to Anne that she marveled anyone took it seriously. She came dangerously close to the brink of asking Miss Aley why a woman her age was still in pursuit of money. She wanted to ask the woman, too, what she had ever bought with money to compensate for the fact she'd never married. Somehow Anne managed to contain these questions, and somehow she managed to rise with reasonable eagerness after Miss Aley had turned from another long inspection of the copper-foil women in their inadequate copperfoil Bikinis. Together, they went to the empty shop between the Indian Arts Shoppe and the Clepsydra Time Center. In the window of the Clepsydra, Mr. Lange took the watchmaker's loupe from his eye and waved. He came outdoors while Miss Aley was rummaging in her handbag for the door key. Anne introduced him to Miss Aley, and Miss Aley said pleasantly, "That's an attractive shop you have, Mr. Lange. You won't recall, of course, but I was prowling around in there one day, admiring your antique clocks."

"As I remember," he said, "you wanted to buy the clock with the Gretchen on the roof. More people want that Gretchen, for some reason."

Miss Aley got the shop door open. "I'm thinking of establishing a gallery here," she told Mr. Lange. "Miss Hendlay and I would be partners."

"Well, there's a lot of interest in art in Santa Fe," Mr. Lange conceded. "But I'd guess it's a risky business if you don't have enough capital."

"Miss Aley operates a gallery in San Francisco, Mr. Lange," Anne explained. "She'd be the brains behind the business."

Mr. Lange surprised her by asking, "Would those statues stay? They're good for business. I'd say that my business has picked up twenty percent since those statues went on display."

"Well," Anne said, "until someone buys them, I suppose they'll stay. Tom has no other place to show them, and they're too good just to poke into a garage or something."

Mr. Lange stood fiddling with his white mustache for a few seconds. He surprised Anne again by asking outright, "Are you making money these days, Miss Hendlay? More than you made before the statues were put out there?"

"According to Nora O'Dell, yes. She keeps track of such things, and she says that our business is up around thirty percent. But I'm not sure we can credit the statues with that. Those busloads of tourists are a help."

"Say the statues increased your business by only ten percent," Mr. Lange argued. "That gives them a real cash value, doesn't it?"

Miss Aley said smoothly, "A novelty that's also art, Mr. Lange, always has a solid cash value. It seems to me that it would be reasonable to make a modest offer to Mr. Zimmerman in the circumstances. Frankly, I've been thinking of calling the gallery The Gallery of the Five Statues. A name like that is just different enough to stick in the memory, and even to attract interest. Suppose we offered Mr. Zimmerman a thousand dollars? I'd put in five hundred dollars, since I'd be getting business identification from those statues."

He nodded and smiled. "I'd put in two hundred and fifty," he said. "As a matter of fact, I like the way he's made those statues. I know something

70

about craftsmanship, you see. The man's a good craftsman as well as a fine artist."

Anne came alive long enough to feel thrilled for Tom Zimmerman. "Count me in," she said. "I'll even waive my customary commission. It's a sale."

Mr. Lange went back to his shop, and Miss Aley and Anne stepped into the empty store. The place had a musty smell, but it was clean and in fairly good condition. They inspected the main room, the storage facilities at the rear, the half-bath. Miss Aley found a chair to sit on. She sat in silence a long time, her pudgy hands folded on her lap, her eyes darting every whichway. Presently she smiled. "Young lady," she confessed, "moments like this always delight me. There's creation in the business world. From nothing, using only a little idea, one creates a business. And if one creates a gallery, a true art gallery, one creates even more—a center of culture in an often uncaring world. Have you decided to enter into partnership with me?"

"It's a problem," Anne told her. The next thing she knew, she was telling the woman all the thoughts that had been troubling her from the moment Robert Lund had driven off yesterday afternoon. Miss Aley listened without interruption. After Anne had run down, the woman shrugged.

"What can anyone advise you?" she queried. "It's a question of deciding, actually, what you hope to extract from life. As a girl, I had the same decision to make—all of us do, really. I lived in a small town in Ohio, in a lovely home in the better section of town. For a while it seemed important to me to be like all the other girls I knew. I fretted over acne, I spent hours doing my hair just so, and I counted every Sunday lost if I didn't have a boy to walk me home after church. Then I was given an album for Christmas that changed everything. Fifty reproductions of paintings that had changed the world—according to the blurb on the book jacket. I was fascinated. So I studied those paintings, and then I studied all the art I could find, and presently I was going to Cleveland whenever I could to roam the museum aisles. I did attend college, but I was an indifferent student of academic subjects. I opened my first gallery in Cleveland a year after my graduation. I did well, but Cleveland wasn't as oriented to art as I thought a city should be. So I sold the gallery and went to San Francisco. I did quite well, And somehow, along the way, it stopped mattering to me if boys noticed me or didn't notice me. I had the world of art, my gallery, a lovely apartment, success."

"Those were enough?"

"Quite enough. I can say this about your relationship with Robert Lund. Whether a person marries or doesn't marry, he must be himself. I'm sure that in marriage theres a molding of two lives

72

in many ways. But deep, deep down, in the core of ourselves, we live forever alone. We have crazy thoughts we share with no one; we have longings, ambitions—well, so many things we can't share with anyone. So you must be yourself even in marriage; not a person living a kind of sham because her husband is somewhat unhappy with the real person you happen to be."

"I've always loved business," Anne said. "I could give up the Sunday afternoon salons, but not business."

"I can assure you, young lady, that this new business will be challenging and profitable. Do you need more time to think things over? I'd like to get started as soon as possible, but I don't want to push you."

While Anne was trying to decide, Nora O'Dell stepped in brightly and briskly. "Mr. Blumberg telephoned to ask about a Mr. Congdon," Nora said. "Such a bear of a man. He growled at me."

Reminded, Anne told her to check the hotels and motels by telephone to find out if a Mr. David Congdon was registered in one of them. Nora groaned but went out to follow orders. Anne told Miss Aley of the deal she'd made with Solomon Blumberg, and at once Miss Aley took a legal-looking document from her handbag. "That being the case," Miss Aley said, "stop being foolish, young lady, and become my partner. You've al-

73

ready made your decision about Robert Lund. If you've agreed to become a buyer for those retail stores, you're committed to remain in business. Very well. This is simply an extension of your business activities and investment."

And that was true, Anne Hendlay thought, so very, very true. . . .

"I'll have my lawyer look over the agreement," she said. Then, smiling, she snapped thumb and forefinger lightly. "And may I have your check for five hundred dollars, please? Poor Tom can use some money."

She had checks from Miss Aley and Mr. Lange when she returned to the shop. She promptly wrote her own check for a thousand dollars, blotted it, and handed the slip of cool green paper to Nora. "Give Tom this loot," she said. "You might tell him that the statues will stay on display practically forever out there."

Nora inhaled deeply.

"And we're in the art business now," Anne went on. "Miss Aley and I are opening The Gallery of the Five Statues next door. We'll cut a door through that wall and operate these two places more or less together. I suppose we'll have to pay you more money?"

"You bet!"

Anne waved her out, amused by the little redhead's anxiety to get going.

"Mr. Congdon's at La Posada over on Castillo Street," Nora reported, stuffing the check into her handbag. "He took one of their suites for a month."

Feeling better, feeling alive again now that she'd made a decision, Anne telephoned David Congdon as soon as Nora had left. He answered the call cheerily and was quite amused when she told him that she was a refugee from the Blumberg retail empire. He arrived at the Arts Shoppe about forty-five minutes later, a tall, well-proportioned fellow of about thirty, his manner assured, his smile broad and somewhat impish.

"Oh, I remember you now," he said as they shook hands. "We met once at headquarters. At the time I was torn between choosing a manager-ship in Kanab, Utah and one in Tucson, Arizona. You gave me a lot of Chamber of Commerce stuff to read, and I chose Utah."

"And now you've flown the coop?"

He glanced with professional interest around the shop. "Your displays could be better," he said genially. "There's too much for the eye to see. We did a study in Salt Lake City last year. We heaped certain counters with merchandise, and we dis-played just a few things on other counters. The uncrowded counters did a better business."

"Maybe it was the merchandise."

"No. After six months we reversed things, and

the counters which had been doing poor business outsold the other counters."

"That's interesting!"

David Congdon sat down and then challenged her with his keen blue eyes. "Mr. Blumberg telephoned you and asked you to send me back?"

"Oh?"

"Now, now, now," he reproved her, "you mustn't try to fool a Blumberg-trained man, Anne. How did you know I was here? How did you know I'd flown the coop?"

"Oh," Anne said casually, "he did mention the matter while he was appointing me buyer of Indian stuff for the chain. He'd like you back, incidentally."

"Sure. And he'll pay me thirty thousand a year. Why not? He wants to move into Wyoming, and he thinks I can make the expansion easier and more profitable for him."

"But you don't want thirty thousand a year?"

"Of course I do! A man's a fool not to earn all the money he can in a society that measures success in terms of money. But I don't want to be a corporation man, you see—a pipsqueak conformist in a gray flannel suit. Look at me! I'm twenty-nine! I've been in that organization for almost thirteen years. Errand boy! Stock boy! Clerk! Management trainee! Manager's assistant! Manager! District manager! State manager! All my

76

working life, don't you see, beginning from the middle of my fifteenth year! What kind of one-sided life is that?"

Anne said, impressed, "You certainly went up through the ranks, David."

He gave a testy wave of his hand. "Nothing remarkable in that," he said grimly. "I'm the boy who never finished high school or went to college. Dates? No time for girls. Ball games? No time for fun. No time for any life outside the corporation. Why wouldn't I have gotten ahead?"

"So what happened?" Anne asked, genuinely curious.

"So one day, near Temple Square in Salt Lake City, I saw the girls in their summer dresses walking along with their scrubbed, nicely dressed fellows. The girls and boys were smiling, having some fun in life. Suddenly I wanted very much to be like those fellows, to be as lucky as those fellows. So I gave my life a good hard-nosed look. Believe it or not, I remembered that you'd quit Blumberg to come here. I even remembered a letter you'd written him about the fun you were having in the most romantic city on earth. So when he called me to Denver and told me I could have Wyoming, I decided that was that. Do you know what will happen to me after Wyoming if I make Wyoming profitable territory? Headquarters! Vice president in charge of Utah, Arizona and California. Then the executive staff. According to Mr. Blumberg, I could be president of the company before I'm fifty."

"This would be bad?"

"When do I live?" he asked bluntly. "Do I wait until I'm fifty to do what I should be doing at twenty-nine?"

"Well, what should you be doing now that you're not doing?"

"How about dinner next Saturday, Anne? I'll dance with you. I may even kiss you! Look. To me there's a huge world completely disassociated from the Blumberg retail empire. I want to see it, to have fun in it. I may even paint. I can paint, you know. Not every well, but it's fun."

Anne thought—she couldn't help it—the poor man.

"It's a date," she said impulsively. "But of course I always eat a ton of garlic."

David Congdon grinned. "Fine. I'll call Mr. Blumberg and tell him you did your best, but it was no go."

Chapter Eight

Walter Sward approved the contract, and Anne signed it. On Saturday morning she and Miss Aley briefed Mona in some detail about their plans, while Mona sat smiling seraphically at the crisp, enamel-blue sky. Mona asked pointblank if they really thought it wise to associate the new gallery with the five statues which had kicked up such a furor. Miss Aley gave them both some insight into her thinking and methods by saying promptly, "The reason I urged that we buy the statues, Miss Yates, was that I expect to benefit from the furor. In a sense, the purchase was a declaration of our policy. We're interested in art—not in censorship. We seek artists, not commercial hacks who'll dance to any tune a buyer pipes. I'm sure we'll not get the work of established artists to handle, but I do think we'll attract the young, sincere strugg-

79

lers. So from the very beginning, you see, The Gallery of the Five Statues will be different."

"What sort of things will you specialize in?"

"Art. Period. If it's art, we'll have it, whether it's conservative or *avant-garde*. We want all periods, all styles—surrealism, cubism, expressionism, surrealistic formalism, representational—"

"And all expressions," Anne added firmly, "whether they're paintings on canvas, sculpture, metalwork, or what-not."

"Girl to girl," Mona said, "I'm having a thing published in the feature section tomorrow about the plans being made by certain ladies of the Plateau Club. They intend to open an Art Arcade, as they call it, near the Plaza. Now you come along with an entirely different concept—a concept in conflict with theirs. Anne, darling, you'll be at war."

"I suppose so, if they're really interested in controlling the art in this region. But they can't hurt me too much, Mona. Why do you think I've become a buyer for Mr. Blumberg? The losses I'll sustain from a boycott by the Plateau Club and its friends will be made good by my commissions. And I think the new gallery will be profitable. Not in the beginning, perhaps, but over a long term."

"You see," Miss Aley said amusedly, "the Art Arcade will be a make-believe business owned and operated by amateurs. I'm sure that the ladies will work quite enthusiastically for a while, but even adults eventually weary of toys. To us, it will be a business. We'll bring knowledge to it, and we'll bring to it the dedication of business people who see a good opportunity to make money."

Mona gave Anne a meaningful look. "You're warned," she said. "I can bat out a story right now —which is what you want me to do, I know. It would appear tomorrow. Once it's appeared, you can't back out gracefully."

"I am as I am," Anne explained simply. "If I'm not worthy as I am, what can I do? I can't change."

Mona spread her hands to indicate that she'd said all she intended to say. She wrote the story, while Anne drove off alone to some nearby pueblos to look for Indian handicrafts suitable for the Blumberg chain. The story was written when Anne returned home late that evening. "Scheduled for tomorrow," Mona said shortly. "Nothing like the feature I've done for the Plateau Club, of course. I didn't have time to equal that feature. But you'll be in a news column, so your readership will be higher."

"Fine."

"About Robert," Mona said slowly, "I do think you ought to make allowances for him. A person is the sum total of his environment, home training, formal education and instincts. If you're what you are, Robert's what he is."

"But I was willing to marry him then and there," Anne pointed out wretchedly. "He did the walking; not I."

"Could be," Mona said, "that this now ruins everything forevermore."

The possibility gave Anne a restless night. Yet seeing the story in the Sunday paper exhilarated her, quickened in her the contentment she always experienced when she was engaged in doing things rather than thinking long thoughts. Suspecting that the story would bring an army of boys and girls to the afternoon salon, she got breakfast in jig time and then went to work to get enough chow ready for the army. Spaghetti and meat balls would be the main fare, she decided—and what about apple pie for dessert? She drove to the Safeway to pick up supplies. For the next two hours she worked, worked harder than even her parents' hired woman had ever worked in the old Idaho farmhouse during harvest time. Mona apparently figured it was a poor household that couldn't afford to support one lady of leisure. Elegant in velveteen capris and a tunic-style blouse, Mona settled down in the living room to read the *Viewer* from page 1 to page 90—not failing to admire her own writings, of course. "I do these things well,"

Mona said happily. "I should be on a big New York City paper, you know."

But it was Mona who graciously went to the door when the bell was rung at around eleven. "Why, Mrs. Lund," she said pleasantly, "how nice of you to call."

Before Anne could even think of pulling her hands out of the pie dough, Mona had brought the woman into the kitchen. 'Smells lovely," Mona complimented the flushed, unpleasantly surprised chef. "You have such a nice hand with sauces, dear."

Mrs. Lund glanced around in some confusion and then took a seat at the dinette table. "I've not made a pie in years," she said after Mona had left them alone. "I did make pies when Robert's father was alive. We had a most expensive cook who excelled at anything related to the *grande cuisine,* but she never did make pies satisfactory to Mr. Lund."

"These characters we feed around here are interested in bulk chow, Mrs. Lund. It doesn't have to be good—just nice and heavy in their stomachs."

"I'm sure, Anne, that you bake a fine pie. I've told Robert more than once that you're an amazingly competent young woman."

Anne worked on at the board.

"I won't bother you overly long," Mrs. Lund said graciously. "I know what it is to be interrupted during preparations for a party. Robert was disturbed, quite disturbed, when he read the story in today's paper about this gallery you propose to open."

"Well," Anne said conversationally, "I'm a bit disturbed myself. It's a new business enterprise for me; I definitely know a good deal more about Indian arts."

"But it's essential to your happiness to open the gallery?"

Mrs. Lund looked at Anne with beautiful hazel eyes so like her son's that Anne was startled when their glances met. She wondered if in time Robert's hair would gray as becomingly as his mother's had. And would he be, under that lovely gray hair, as youthful as Mrs. Lund seemed to be right now?

"It always makes me unhappy," Mrs. Lund said, "when a man and a woman representative of different social levels, different cultures, really, decide they're in love and ought to marry. Things become—well, sticky. Values differ. Aspirations differ. Though they think they communicate with one another, they really do not."

Anne said defensively, "Yet once upon a time, Mrs. Lund, some man or some woman in the Lund family went out and earned the money and the position for future generations. I can't really see anything shameful in working for a living as I work."

"You see?" Mrs. Lund asked. "You've entirely missed the point. Yet I'm talking in English and in simple terms. My son's wife could and ought to be a figure of importance in the city, a civic influence, a social leader, a cultural force. I dislike to sound regal, but it does seem grubby to me when people who have sufficient resources labor so diligently for acquisitions they don't require."

"Would Robert abandon his financial business, Mrs. Lund, if I insisted?"

Mrs. Lund grimaced delicately. "Now you're being childish, of course. Men must do something with their time. Moreover, the business isn't conducted to make a profit, although I'm sure there are profits. The service Robert performs for our friends is a useful one, an obligation he thinks he ought to meet."

"I think the gallery will be useful to my friends, Mrs. Lund. But I do have to say that I'm interested in profits."

Mrs. Lund rose, a tall, slender woman who was dressed and groomed as if for an afternoon informal social at which she expected to be scrutinized closely and even critically. "You must understand," she said softly, "that I would support my friends of the Plateau Club in any effort they made to advance the cultural interests of Santa Fe."

"I understand," Anne said gently. "I appreciate your making this visit to tell me that."

Mrs. Lund inclined her head in a brief nod and stepped toward the door. Not able to accompany her, her hands covered with dough, Anne called for Mona to do the honors. After Mrs. Lund had left, Anne worked the dough into the pie tins and then went on to see to the fillings. Although there was ample opportunity during the next several hours to discuss the subject of Mrs. Lund's visit with Mona, she thrust the subject from her mind and concentrated wholeheartedly upon her plans to make the salon a complete success from the standpoint of gallery owners who needed artists as much as artists needed gallery owners. She decided to say nothing about The Gallery of the Five Statues until after chow. She then decided not to make a formal pitch for support, as such, but merely to answer any questions the boys and girls had. She would assume that the gallery would be successful, and play it cool!

Her plan worked for only a half-hour, though. Peter Underwood came into the patio with a cluster of admiring models at around two-thirty, just late enough to make an entrance but not so late as to miss chow. And Peter had interesting news to report. "Kids," Peter bragged, "I'm loaded. I didn't know they'd minted so much dinero in this country. If I had a hundred bucks more, I'd have four thousand in the old sock."

The effect was electric.

Peter took time out to pat the face of a model who said she was sure he'd want to celebrate his success by buying her a divine seersucker dress she'd seen in a store. He then elaborated for the benefit of his colleagues: "We've got it made, you bright people, you. The Plateau Club gals want a freight car of stuff. Anne, I could kiss you! They're so eager to get the jump on your new gallery that they're waving money all over the place."

Anne managed to keep her temper. "So sweet of you to come to our salon, Peter, to make a pitch for the Art Arcade. I must do the same favor for you one of these days. But eat, eat, eat. In this house, a guest is always treated tenderly."

Of the thirty or so artists in attendance, about ten showed an interest in exploiting the Plateau Club's anxiety to get the jump on The Gallery of the Five Statues. "Not to offend you," one apologized to Anne, "but I can use some loot."

"Fine with me," Anne said cheerfully. She made a place for herself between two girls by squeezing her hips between their shoulders and allowing gravity to do the rest. She tackled her spaghetti and meat balls heartily, loving the food, loving the delighted expressions of her guests. When she could do so without seeming to make an issue of the matter, she said lightly to Peter, "Did you sell them any nudes or other examples of artistic immorality?"

"Landscapes, dear girl. I've gotten orders for several more. Mrs. Staunton was gracious enough to tell me exactly what's wanted. Very nice."

His reference to Mrs. Staunton had been a mistake. "Real big of her," a cubist said, "to tell an artist what's art and what isn't. Saves a lot of wear and tear on the creative mind."

"I love money," Peter said matter-of-factly. "If they want to give me all that lovely money, that's their business."

"You actually were paid thousands of dollars, Peter?" Anne asked. "Most unusual for a gallery to buy work outright for resale."

Her deliberately mocking tone bothered him. "Well, no," he muttered, "I don't have the cash. They did advance me a few hundred dollars, and they are planning to ask a thousand apiece for my things. But that's as good as money in the bank, isn't it? All those wealthy women!"

Anne didn't make the obvious remark, liking gay Peter too well for that. She did say, however, "At The Gallery of the Five Statues, folks, we'll have a policy of letting you paint what you choose and of exhibiting anything and everything our selection committee tells us is worthy of display.

We'll sell the works for a twenty-five percent commission. And we *won't* hand out advances, not being rich."

Peter said plaintively, "You'll have to do better than that, you know. If you can't top the Art Arcade, you've had it."

"But what do you do," Anne asked, "when the women have found something more fashionable than art to play with? Or what do you do, Peter, with a surrealistic landscape if Mrs. Staunton informs you that the Plateau Club disapproves of surrealism?"

The argument grew hot and heavy after that. Sides were lined up against each other within minutes, some shouting that sales were all that mattered and others shouting that if you painted to order, you were just a two-bit commercial artist who ought to be ashamed.

Around six in the evening, Anne served the apple pie and coffee.

Around eight in the evening, voices beginning to be hoarse now, people demanded more coffee and whatever had been left in the spaghetti pot.

It was midnight before the last couple went off along Canyon Road, still arguing about the meaning and value of art.

Mona nodded when she turned from the gate. "Nice tactics," she complimented Anne. "Even I was impressed by the fact you made no official pitch."

But Anne wasn't sure that she'd brought it off. The Plateau Club, she suspected, would be tougher competition than she'd thought. They could afford to give cash advances, after all.

Chapter Nine

David Congdon settled down with the afternoon newspaper in the spacious living room of the cottage-suite he'd rented for the spring and summer. Although the grounds of La Posada were located in a busy section of Santa Fe, he had the illusion of being in the country. The thick, plastered adobe walls reduced the noise of the city to a faint hum. Birds frisked in the apple trees visible through the several windows. A butterfly came to rest on one of the panes and spread its wings to the sun. Every now and again a breeze stirring outside sent apple blossoms flurrying to the ground like snow. David wondered idly if it ever did snow in Santa Fe. It probably did, he thought, for the city was situated seven thousand feet above sea level, and there were mountains all around. The city must be magnificent in snow, he thought. With its ancient buildings and Spanish-territorial style of architecture, it probably had an old-world charm in snow.

The newspaper had only two items that interested him. On page 6 the establishment of The Gallery of the Five Statues was announced in a quarter-page ad. His attention to the ad was attracted by line drawings of five grotesque women in inadequate Bikinis. He recalled that he'd seen the monstrosities in the patio of the Indian Arts Shoppe, so he read the announcement and was quite interested to learn that Miss Anne Hendlay was one of the proprietors.

The second interesting item was bold-printed halfway down the *Arts Today* column written by Mona Yates. The item was built around a prediction that this would be a happy spring and summer for all artists and art lovers, because the fierce competition between the Art Arcade proposed by the Plateau Club and The Gallery of the Five Statues would assure many exhibitions and sales.

David grinned, for it was obvious between the lines that Mona Yates expected the competition to be sanguinary. A cat fight, David thought, was always interesting to watch. Women fought under different rules from those men used. Moreover, women were more resourceful. So fur always flew beautifully for as long as the fight lasted, and the fight always lasted until one or the other was plain dead. Women never compromised as men did. Emotional always, they transformed even business conflicts into highly personal wars. Fun for the spectators if not for the participants.

Intrigued, David put the paper on the table and hustled to his bedroom to dress for the dinner date with Anne Hendlay. He put on a charcoal-gray suit, a sober necktie, a fedora. Although he was a good hour and a half early, he set off jauntily for the Indian Arts Shoppe. In the patio, he saw that the five statues had been moved to encourage people to go by the windows of all the shops in the compound. David approved this for business reasons, but he did think that the total effect of the display had been blunted by the separation of the statues from one another. Whistling, he stepped into the Indian Arts Shoppe. He found Anne Hendlay and a cute little redhead taking Indian things from cases and checking them for obvious flaws. He grinned at the fetching picture Anne Hendlay made sitting there on the floor, her legs bunched under her. "The more things change," he joshed, "the more they stay the same. I used to make such checks for Blumberg."

Her eyes danced an invitation for him to give two working girls a hand. Amused. David put his hat and jacket on a chair in the railed-off office section. "You use the Blumberg check-off method, I hope?" he asked.

"Naturally," Anne assured him. "You handle the lists while we count and inspect. All this stuff is intended for Mr. Blumberg. I know how tough you managers can be, especially when you're accepting a new line for the first time."

"The dolls," he said kindly, "should be a lively item. A good many adults collect dolls. They're usually ethnic collections, you know. Features and costumes must be authentic."

"These are. I have dolls representative of seven different tribes."

"How do you acquire them?"

Anne chuckled. "Now that's a long story, David," she answered, "and we do have this work to do."

Dutifully, he got the lists together and made check-offs as the inventory progressed. They made good progress despite the interruptions of customers. The last doll was inspected and checked off close to five o'clock. David looked through his lists and said, impressed: "Only thirteen rejects. These Indians know something about quality control, don't they?"

"Naturally. They've been doing these handcrafts for many centuries. If they're folk artists, they're artists in every sense of the word."

The cute little redhead emptied the cash register and laid the money on the desk to be counted and put into the night-deposit bank bag. David was impressed by the day's receipts. "If you work on a forty per cent markup," he said, "you've made a bundle, haven't you?'

"I don't have a standard markup," Anne told him. "I tried to use the Blumberg method in that area, too, but it just didn't work. So many of these items I sell are popular only because they're inexpensive. If I took more than fifteen percent on them, people would pass them by."

The closed bank bag was tossed to the diminutive redhead. The girl called a cheery good night and went off jauntily. She closed the door behind her, and she closed the wrought-iron patio gate as well. A flick of some wall switches, and most of the shop was in darkness.

"I couldn't primp," Anne Hendlay explained apologetically, "because I knew these things would be delivered late this afternoon. I hate to keep men waiting to buy me a dinner, but if you want a properly primped companion, I'll have to drive you to my home first and park you in the living room with Mona Yates."

"The art critic? I've just read her column."

"That's my Mona. I wish, darn it, that she'd not

94

made that allusion to fierce competition. A lot of the younger artists around here will develop exaggerated ideas of their worth."

"You look charming," David said. He put on his jacket, smoothed his hair. "Why don't we just walk to the Palace from here? They serve excellent dinners."

"Fine."

He thought, for some reason, that he ought to say more. "You mustn't get the idea," he said, "that I expect a big show from a woman. That stuff I told you about girls in their summer dresses —I'm not the sort of person, believe it or not, who measures a woman in terms of her appearance."

"I didn't think that," Anne said gently. "But a girl does like to look nice when she's being taken out."

They walked off toward the Palace a few minutes later. The sunset was making long shadows wherever they looked in the city. In the sunset, they followed a curving street past the Cathedral of St. Francis. Pigeons were fluttering about the belfry, and Anne, her eyes glowing, stopped to look at them awhile. Slim, lovely, just a scrap of femininity before the massive building, she gave a sigh that touched David oddly and inspired him to take her hand. "I understand," he said, "that the Bishop Lamy who planned and built that cathedral was the principal character in Wilma Cather's novel, *Death Comes for the Archbishop*. One of the things I love about Santa Fe is this blend of history, fiction and fact."

"You're a dreadful sentimentalist, David, aren't you?"

He gave that thought as they moved on again. "Well," he admitted, "I suppose so. I suppose that's one of the reasons I couldn't stay with Blumberg."

"You want people to be people, and you want to be yourself?"

"Yes."

"But business is important, too. And big business does have to use big business methods."

"Why did you quit Blumberg, Anne?"

She laughed softly, and now the wistfulness in her eyes was replaced by a joyous sparkle. "I had to prove something to myself," she confided. "Working with Mr. Blumberg was both a privilege and a thrill, don't misunderstand me. You couldn't work as secretary for a nicer or more understanding man. But all his fulminations against women! I felt I could be a good manager, and I felt I deserved a chance. But I couldn't budge him an inch, and then I began to wonder if he was right, if a woman could really operate a retail store as he thinks they should be operated. Eventually, I decided I'd just have to find out who was right."

"You both are," David said. He held the door

open after they'd reached the Palace. He waited until after they'd been seated in the beautiful dining room, and then he went on: "A woman can't manage a Blumberg Variety Store as Mr. Blumberg wants because much of the work—especially in the smaller towns—is physical. But certain types of stores, such as the one you have, can be managed very successfully by women."

"You're probably correct," she conceded. "I'm told by Mr. Blumberg that you're usually correct, by the way. Yes, I've been in touch with him again. He has two messages for you. First, a Beulah Cummings of Cummings, Utah wants you to stop being silly. The other message is that he'll give you thirty-five thousand a year."

He never lost his composure. "All right," he said: "You've given me the messages. Now, then, shall we enjoy ourselves?"

A waitress came for their orders, and eventually they were served a fine roast beef dinner. At the end of the room, adding a final extra touch to the joy of eating such grand food in the sumptuous scarlet and white setting, a three-piece string ensemble played delightful music. The lovely brunette reacted to it all as David had rather hoped she would. Eyes and facial muscles softened. She lowered her guard. She began to talk not of business but of the grand life she'd found in Santa Fe. "Of course," she said laughingly, "I know far too many men and women who make a point of being noncomformist. Those who've been educated properly pretend otherwise. Those least able to follow the arts are the loudest talkers about the need for artistic excellence. But they're fine people. Once they've accepted you, it's impossible to have an unhappy or lonely life in Santa Fe."

David said eagerly, "I'd like to meet them, if I could."

"To savor the romantic life of old Santa Fe in enchanted New Mexico?"

David explained, embarrassed, "That was written to Mr. Blumberg to discourage him from trying to keep me in the organization. No. What I'm after in Santa Fe is my own life, my own identity."

She nodded, and with the nod she told him this was the most successful date he'd ever had in his life. It sort of awed him that this woman, this young, beautiful, rather self-contained woman, could understand him so well so quickly. . . .

Chapter Ten

Mona's comments about "fierce competition" had been read, studied, and absorbed by far too many of the artists who attended the salon the following afternoon. Although work was usually brought to the salon for exhibition and constructive criticism, not a one of the boys and girls had brought a thing with him. There were no apologies. The boys and girls ate and drank quite as if they thought it natural and proper that they be entertained at someone else's expense. All the chatter, of course, involved the fine year of sales each was anticipating. Lest the message not be understood, Peter Underwood summed up the general thinking by saying, after dessert, "The worm has turned around here, Anne, my love. Crude though it may sound, we men and women of genius expect to get ours. No tickee, no shirtee. Clever?"

Not blaming any of them, Anne put on an easy,

friendly smile to indicate that the message hadn't offended her. She did make a point, however, of waylaying Loretta Turley as the boys and girls headed for home around midnight. Holding the gay blonde beauty by the hand, Anne led Loretta upstairs to her bedroom. She had Loretta sit on Mona's bed, and then she asked, "Are they talking, Loretta, or are they really serious?"

Loretta thrust her legs straight out. "I adore my legs," she said, "don't you? I always marvel that these people refuse to paint me exactly as I am. I'm as God made me. I think it's impertinent of people to think they can improve upon God's creation."

"The reason I hope that they're not serious, Loretta, is that they'll hurt themselves rather than me. If they want to paint what they're told to paint, that's their business. But they won't be artists if they do that. They'll be paid commercial hacks."

Loretta's luminous gray eyes danced. "After all," she said, "you've not really made a serious offer yet. Your commission may be ten percent lower, but you keep your money in a bank. I'm opposed to banks as a matter of principle."

"No advances," Anne said wearily. "We don't have millions of dollars behind us."

"People do have to eat. It can be sickeningly

long between sales. A man or a girl can actually starve between sales."

Anne sat on the opposite bed. A cool breeze was stirring the curtains, but the breeze seemed to have no cooling effect upon her. She considered the lovely, faintly heart-shaped face with its creamy skin and cherry-red lips. A different tack was indicated by the model's cocky smile, so Anne took a different tack.

"Peter got several advances," she said. "Has he done the paintings yet?"

"What paintings?"

"I'm sure that in exchange for the advances on the things they've taken, the Art Arcade has committed him to do other things for them. Right?"

"Oh, that. Well, they did, that's true."

"Has he even begun the new paintings?"

"No, not that I know of. But you know Peter. As long as he has money in his pocket, he never works."

"What does he do when the advances run out? He can't do other work for me while he's committed to do work for them."

Loretta asked indignantly, "Are you trying to use scare tactics on me?"

With all the exquisite grace of a panther, Loretta was off and running for the door. A few seconds later, Anne heard the downstairs door slam shut, too.

But Loretta had of course taken the words with her. . . .

On Tuesday morning, Walter Sward asked Anne in a strange tone of voice to come to his office right away. When Anne got there, puffing after some fast walking, she found Mrs. Elmo Staunton seated beside the lawyer's desk. Mrs. Staunton announced with considerable satisfaction, "The Art Arcade has decided to sue you, young lady, for a substantial sum of money."

Walter made soothing sounds, but Mrs. Staunton wasn't to be mollified. "How dare you suggest to anyone," she asked Anne, "that the Plateau Club is viciously indifferent to human welfare?"

Anne sat calmly and folded her hands on her lap. Regardless of what was said to her, she decided, she'd not be rude, unkind, or even aggressive. This was the same woman, after all, who did a great deal of good for a great many underprivileged people in the city. Also, she'd always liked Mrs. Staunton, just as she'd always admired her.

"You see?" Mrs. Staunton asked Wlater. "She has no defense."

Not smiling, Walter said: "It's come to Mrs. Staunton's attention, Anne, that you've questioned certain arrangements she'd made with certain artists. Specifically, you've suggested that the Art Arcade would be heartless in its dealings with any artist who neglected to deliver paintings in conformance with the terms of a signed contract."

"Not guilty," Anne said promptly. "I merely reminded Loretta Turley that a friend of hers, Peter Underwood, couldn't do work for me until after he'd met his commitments to the Art Arcade. That was a statement of business fact, Walter."

"And these statements that we'll presume to tell the artists what to paint and what not to paint?"

"What's Peter painting, Mrs. Staunton?"

"Landscapes. Magnificent landscapes."

"Suppose he submitted a nude? He does nudes extraordinarily well, according to critics."

"There's no market for nudes these days."

"Then if Peter does a nude and you reject it, may he give it to us without incurring your wrath?"

"My dear young lady, we naturally expect that the artists we push will favor us with their total production. It would be perfectly idiotic, now wouldn't it, for us to build Peter up so that a competitor could capitalize on his fame?"

"Then, in effect, you're telling them what to paint and what not to paint. If they disobey, you dump them. If you dump them, all the ladies of the Plateau Club will boycott their work."

"Well, we **do** have the right to our standards, Anne Hendlay. This may be a socialistic country

103

now, but we do retain the right to maintain our standards."

Anne rose and smiled at Walter. "If they wish to use me," she said, "Let them do so, by all means. Anything else?"

Mrs. Staunton snapped, "You're a very foolish young woman, Hendlay. For a reason I'll never entirely understand, you've been given an opportunity few girls on your social level are given to make something of themselves. I actually volunteered to aid you in making the transition from the status of working girl to—"

"Mrs. Staunton, I'm sure you mean well, but we're at opposite poles in this matter of art. To you, this is a little game to be played for a year or so and then dropped. To the artists, it's a way of life, and to me it's a means of life. Well, I can't let you become the arbiter of art in Santa Fe, nor can any of the other gallery owners. You'd kill art, real art, within a year."

There being nothing more to add, Anne left.

But there was more to come. . . .

On Thursday, looking worried, Peter Underwood came to the patio with a landscape that reeked of oils and turp. After Anne and Nora had admired it for a time, Peter said generously, "You may have it to show, dear love, in exchange for a three-hundred-dollar advance."

"Go away," Anne said promptly. "You've just

finished that, Peter, and you know it. Take it to the Art Arcade. If they reject it, get the rejection in writing and then bring it back. I'll hang it in exchange for exactly nothing in the form of an advance."

Peter left grumpily. Apparently he spread the word among his colleagues, because no one, no one at all, showed up on Sunday for the salon. Annoyed, looking at all the Mexican food going to waste, Anne telephoned David Congdon and Walter Sward and Nora and told them to bring healthy appetites. Nora surprised her by saying in a strangely cool voice, "I'm not in the mood for any kind of a party, Miss Hendlay, thank you so much." David and Walter came, however, Walter to eat and David to feast his eyes, presumably, upon the two beautiful women whom Walter, the glutton, more or less ignored.

Anne was interested in watching the way Mr. David Congdon went to work on Mona Yates.

"You write a meaty column, Mona," David began. "I'm not sure that I appreciate surrealism as much as you do, but you make it seem fairly comprehensive to me."

"Nice of you to say so, darling. I'm not entirely sure that I'm comprehensible even to myself. Too bad these idiots didn't come today. We having some articulate artists, I'll have you know, who can explain even cubism so it can be understood."

Anne sank onto the couch beside Walter. He gave her pleasure of a kind, for while he didn't talk, he did eat with a flattering gusto. He ate four enchiladas, three tacos, and five heaping table-spoons of frijoles. He refreshed himself with a tall bottle of Seven-Up, and then returned to the buffet to refill his plate.

"To me," Anne heard David say to Mona, "the epitome of beauty is a girl in a summer dress, her face joyous as she walks with her beloved. I try to paint such girls. No, I'm not an artist; merely a dabbler. I got one of those paint-by-number kits from the stock at the store one year, and I fiddled around with it. After a bit, I dropped the number guide. I like the freedom of just splashing color where I will. But one girl I did is quite good. Entirely an accident. She just arrived on the canvas, don't ask me why."

Walter smiled faintly when he came back to Anne's side. "Callow sort of guy, isn't he?" Walter asked. "I wonder what hermitage you plucked him from."

"But nice in a confused sort of way."

"The longer I practice law," Walter told her, "the more I doubt that anyone can be nice. By the way, I bumped into Robert Lund yesterday. He was giving a golf ball a lick on the practice tee. We discussed the client with the wart on her nose. The reason he fired her, he explained, is that this very rich client was reminded by that wart of a hateful nurse she had as a child. Very kind man, Robert Lund. He offered to find the girl a job and give her a few dollars to soothe her feelings."

Across the room, sitting at Mona's lovely feet now, David Congdon said, "But beauty's an inner quality, really, an almost spiritual gift a woman either has or doesn't have. I know a woman in Utah named Beulah Cummings. Most men gape in admiration when they see her. But I find that when I gaze into her eyes I see only vanity—and vanity is never beautiful, is it?"

Walter gave Anne a polite little nudge. "I have a message from Robert," he announced. "He'll forgive you the silliness of the gallery if you'll close it."

"We've not even opened it, Walter."

"Mrs. Staunton won't sue you, incidentally. After you left, we had a plain talk. She doesn't adore you, but she won't sue you."

The doorbell rang. Anne answered, being less heavily engaged with masculinity, and it was just as well, because the telegram was for her. The Indian things had arrived safely in Denver and had been test-marketed in selected Colorado stores. Sales results indicated a lively interest in low-priced Indian art as distinct from low-priced Indian junk. So would Miss Anne Hendlay invest fifty thousand dollars of the company's money in more dolls, pottery, carvings and such?

And where was David Congdon?

Concealing her elation, Anne returned to Walter's side. She gave him the telegram and accepted his congratulations.

"I'm afraid," Walter said, "that you can really grow, Anne. Even if you don't marry Robert Lund, you may end up rich."

"I don't care a hang about the money, Walter. I do love to be doing things, though. Robert doesn't understand that. Well, who wants to be his mother, or Mrs. Elmo Staunton?"

"If you married me," Walter said, "I'd let you make me as rich as you wanted to make me."

There was that, Anne thought. And there was yonder idiot, too, trying so hard to make her jealous that even Mona was more amused than vexed.

Just possibly, Anne wondered, it was time a girl found someone other than a demanding Robert Lund to moon about.

So. Mr. David Congdon honed for romance, did he?

Chapter Eleven

Cute little Nora was cool throughout the succeed-
ing week. She did her work meticulously, and she
even helped Miss Aley at odd moments in the
shop next door; but all this was done with minimal
conversation and without the customary gaiety
that had always made her a joy to have on the premises. Not being entirely naive, Anne imagined
that their strained relations were the result of her
decision not to compete for artists either by offering them advances or by providing them a guaran-
teed gallery they could turn to in the event the Art
Arcade displeased them in any way. Anne was
sorry that Nora didn't see things her way, and
once or twice she was tempted to explain the facts
of business life to the redhead. She curbed the im-
pulse, however, reasoning that a girl as interested
in an artist as Nora was would find the objectivity
of business impossible to understand or accept.

At the end of the week Miss Aley suggested that June fifteenth would be as good a date as any to establish as their opening date. Miss Aley had drawings of the gallery she'd planned, and she'd also made color notes of the highpoints of the general decor. To a girl accustomed to operating a cluttered store, the layout of the proposed gallery seemed highly wasteful of good space. Anne pointed that out at once, her Blumberg-trained mind shuddering at the prospect of trying to make a good net income under the handicaps imposed by so much unproductive space. Miss Aley heard her out, smiling faintly, her own eyes twinkling. Then Miss Aley proceeded to give her her first lesson in the art of managing an art gallery.

"We won't be selling sausages here, Anne, or any other type of low-cost item that gets you a profit only if sold in volume. We're selling beauty, beauty that must be presented in a proper environment. There must be sufficient space between paintings so that the eye isn't distracted from one thing to the other. Each painting must be seen and appreciated as a single unit. That way, the prospective customer can study it thoroughly and decide if he does or doesn't want it in his home or office. The more distractions you have, the fewer sales you have."

"But these totally empty wall panels, Miss Aley!"

The plump woman nodded. She went to the storage room, bulky in her pink smock but walking lightly and even gracefully. She returned carrying a large seascape. She went to one of the wall panels and hung the painting at about eye level and stepped back. "Now it isn't empty," she said. "These empty panels would be display panels for paintings the customer seems especially interested in. In other words, he makes a few choices. You or Nora then hang the paintings one by one on an empty panel up front. Now a final decision can be made."

"People can't just say they like this or that and buy?"

"Not really. A painting is a luxury item, you know. It may represent an investment of thousands of dollars. A proper atmosphere, proper display, a proper respect for each painting, a proper respect for each customer . . . these things are important."

Anne said, awed: "You said *thousands* of dollars?"

Miss Aley indicated the seascape. It was an exciting painting of an ocean in turmoil under a slate-gray sky. If one looked at the painting longer than just a few seconds, the ocean seemed to move and swirl and splash foam about with incredible force.

"The woman who painted that," Miss Aley

111

said, "is considered to be a genius in the rich little seacoast town she lives in out in California. Her paintings sell regularly there for about four thousand each. And that's not much money, really, when you consider she averages two paintings a year."

Anne gulped. When she could speak, she conceded: "You'd have to sell a lot of sausages to rack up four thousand dollars."

Anne approved the plans and the decor without further discussion.

The following week the renovation of the shop next door was begun. Anne had four contractors come to bid for the job, and she finally gave the job to a Mr. Gonzalez who'd been recommended by Mr. Lange. The same afternoon an electrician came to install a new wiring system, overhead lights and wall lights. After the wiring had been done, Mr. Gonzalez came with an assistant to install creamy ceiling tile and to line all the walls with smooth-faced plyboard. Next an upholsterer came to line the walls with a soft batting over which he drew a canvas liner skin tight. The job was long and slow, primarily because of all the electrical wall sockets, but toward the end of May the final wall covering was put on: a rough-textured beige that had the patina of long-used sterling silver.

David's reaction to the renovation was interesting. He came swinging into the patio just as the wall upholsterer was leaving. He stuck his head into the gallery, and then he quirked his eyebrows and walked all the way in. "Very elegant," he pronounced the walls. "Is it a place of business, though, or milady's boudoir in embryo?"

"That's the Blumberg training talking," Anne teased. "But Mr. Blumberg in effect sells sausages."

"You should make here the net we made last year in Salt Lake City."

"We'll probably not even come close," Anne said ruefully. "But in this business, according to Miss Aley, atmosphere is everything."

"For what the suggestion's worth, why don't you get one of those Spanish style iron chandeliers from Fred Vicks? I was at his place the other day. He has some beauties. This place could use a solid chunk of craftsmanship right now. It strikes me as being too precious."

It was, Anne thought, an idea.

With David, she went across Canyon Road that evening to Fred's barnlike studio behind his house. The red-haired gorilla was working, stripped to the waist, at his little forge. Face smudged, sweat gleaming on his skin, he bawled to them to wait a few minutes, and then he pulled a length of metal from the forge and gave it a dozen or so wallops with his hand sledge. It was ten minutes before he was satisfied that he had the piece he wanted. He gave the piece a final heating and then transferred it with tongs to a tempering solution. "These rich people," he complained, taking them into his little office. "They wait until the last minute; then they want you to make a masterpiece in two days. I'm working on an elegant wrought-iron gate for Mrs. Staunton. They've decided to knock out part of the fence and put an entrance to the Art Arcade on Pedro Alley."

Fred lit a cigarette and smoked for a time. He then said embarrassedly, "I hope you're not here, Anne, to get something for the gallery. I do a lot of work for the ladies of the Plateau Club. I can live comfortably on the yearly income I get from that work. Liking to feed my family regularly, I wouldn't want to risk losing that connection."

"I understand. I just thought we'd like to buy a big chandelier."

"The cheapest one I've got," Fred said promptly, "would cost ten thousand, and I wouldn't be able to deliver it for five years."

It hurt, really hurt, hurt so sharply that Anne gasped. Meeting Fred's impenitent gaze, Anne wondered if she'd actually made any friends during her three years in Santa Fe. This man, she thought resentfully, had borrowed money from her, had eaten at least a hundred meals at her house, and had even come there many times to all but cry on her shoulder during the difficult days of courting the Nan he'd finally married. And who'd driven Nan to the hospital that wild night the baby had been born?

After the hurt came anger, an anger so savagely, intense that Anne quivered with it. But she could control her tongue if not her other muscles. "All right," she said simply, rising. "We'll forget the order; we'll forget other things."

"When can I call for that stuff of mine you have on consignment in the Indian Arts Shoppe?"

"Tomorrow will be convenient, Fred. Either around eight-thirty or just after five."

Back in the patio, with only David there to see, Anne had a different reaction. In a queer, almost hysterical way, she began to laugh.

"Easy," David Congdon said soothingly. "It never helps."

"But it's so comical," Anne cried feverishly, "don't you see? I'm supposed to have business brains. But for years and years I've been clipped by artists who aren't supposed to have business brains at all."

"Nonsense." David made her sit on a marble bench before the fountain and pool. Overhead, a crescent moon glittered, and in the moonlight the fountain seemed to be tossing diamonds into the soft spring air. "As Mr. Blumberg's manual says in a dozen places, there's no place in business for

115

sentiment. The man has a family to support. He can't sell as much to you as he can to the ladies of the Plateau Club. He may think that you're right and they're wrong, but he has to protect his market."

Another thought made Anne laugh all over again. "And you actually came here, David, to savor the romance of life in old Santa Fe in enchanted New Mexico!"

David kissed her mouth, just like that, so quickly it was over before she quite realized what was happening. "Romance is a girl in a summer dress," David said, "don't you remember? I learned a long time ago not to expect to find it in the business world."

Anne made a prodigious effort to get hold of herself.

"Would you laugh," David asked, "if I told you I've never done that before? I don't mean I've never kissed a woman. But never so impulsively. I'm not an impulsive man."

"I won't die."

"This girl Beulah Cummings that Mr. Blumberg told you about—she's the most beautiful woman you'll ever see. The Cummings family owns the town of Cummings. They mine talc and other minerals, including gold. I'm supposed to marry her. Mr. Cummings has said so, Beulah has said so. I'm a solid man of business, you see, a

116

suitable man to train for an executive position in the family enterprise."

"But you told me—"

"I've never really had a date as such before I came here. When you meet Beulah, and I'm sure you will, you'll understand what I mean. With Beulah, a date is a command performance. A manager of a Blumberg store never offends important people. So I saw a life unfolding for me that I didn't want. And here I am. And there's romance in Santa Fe, I'm afraid. You're wrong to claim there isn't."

"Or maybe," Anne asked, "it's all illusion?"

She left David there, thinking it was just as well.

Chapter Twelve

Mona agreed it was probably best to cancel the salons for a while, so until The Gallery of the Five Statues was ready to open, Anne spent her weekends out in Indian country. She took David with her the first weekend and was delighted to notice that he loved the sweet, vast land on sight. She let him accompany her into the various pueblos to look over stock and to listen to her bargain for the things she wanted. But the next weekend she took Walter Sward with her, deliberately trying to establish in David's mind the realization she wasn't a dream girl in a summer dress who existed to give him a taste of hail romance. The weekend with Walter wasn't nearly as much fun, though. Walter was much too serious. Walter found the Indians dirty, the pueblos wretched; and on Sunday morning, when he came out of his motel room three doors up from hers, he gazed with considerable distaste at the upthrust of stone from the plains that had given the town of Shiprock its name. "I'm not an ardent admirer of nature in the raw," Walter growled. "To me, a city like Santa Fe represents a peak achieved by a civilized society. All this empty land! I like fine shops, fine restaurants, fine museums, that sort of thing."

"Well," Anne said mollifyingly, "there are tastes and tastes."

The third weekend she went alone, and that seemed the best weekend of all. She spent ten thousand dollars of Mr. Blumberg's money and two thousand dollars of her own. That Saturday evening she slept in one of the pueblos, sharing a room with a young Indian woman who'd decided that college wasn't for her or life away from the pueblo, either.

"I hated college," Juana said. "Life in a pueblo is warm, rich, exciting. Life in college was so cold. The girls were sweet. I made some divine friends, in fact. But everything was so empty."

"What's a full life?" Anne challenged.

Juana smiled and rolled onto her stomach and propped her head up with her hands. "This is a full life," she said. "I'm with my family in my home, I earn enough money as a waitress in La Fonda, I see my friends, I drive the men half out of their minds.

"You're ambitious to marry, is that it?"

"Not ambitious. You Caucasians make too much of ambition. What I want is life in the natural order of things. As a little girl, I ran around this place in the warm sun, and I played with my friends, and I was happy. Sometimes we'd sit and splash in the creek. Other times we'd play house or just sing and dance in front of the radio. Then I grew older, and I was as deliciously confused about life and my relationship to society as any other teen-age girl. Then college . . . now this. In the natural order of things, a man will behold in me all he ever dreamed a woman could be. Then we'll marry, and the children will come. See? I'm not ambitious for this; I'm simply living happily while I await the inevitable, natural order of things."

Anne had what she thought was an excellent idea. "I could use another girl in my shop, Juana. I'm expanding, and my business is very good. I'll want to spend less time waiting on customers and more time buying. I'd start you with sixty-five dollars a week. Nora, my only assistant right now, is earning seventy-five and will be raised next week to eighty-five."

Juana smiled prettily. "Oh, no," she protested. "All the air around you is charged up with ambition. It isn't peaceful air or happy air. I noticed the same thing at the college. I used to watch the girls hurry so and fret so, and I often wondered what the fuss was all about."

"But getting ahead does have its good points," Anne argued. "I used to live on a farm. We were never hungry, but we weren't in a position to buy all the things we wanted, either. Now I have a nice business, a lovely home, beautiful clothes."

"Still, the air around you isn't peaceful. My mother used to tell me outdoors that to be what you are is to be everything that matters. A mountain does not expect to be a trout. A bird does not expect to be a snorting bull. When I sit outdoors and am Juana, I feel in harmony with the universe, and I look up and smile gratefully at the Virgin Mary."

The words lingered in Anne's mind as she drove back to Santa Fe the next day, and she suspected that possibly those words were the best things she was taking home with her from that particular trip. She passed the words along to Mona as they sat out on the patio in the warm evening air, eating a supper consisting of cold cuts and salad. Mona grinned lazily. "I subscribe to that philosophy forthwith," she announced. "It's so unstrenuous to be oneself. And I adore that bit about the natural order of things. News! In the natural order of things, Robert Lund came hat in hand this afternoon in quest of an utterly unreasonable brunette."

Anne discovered, to her dismay, that just the name of the brute could quicken her pulse.

"I'm to tell you, Anne, that you've come to the Rubicon in your wanderings. Mrs. Lund has ranged herself solidly in the ranks behind Mrs. Elmo Staunton. To oppose the efforts of Mrs. Staunton and the Plateau Club to enhance the cultural life of Santa Fe would be to oppose Mrs. Lund, in effect. Tomorrow, if you indeed open the gallery, you'll have crossed the Rubicon."

Anne started to rise, thinking a telephone chat with Robert was in order.

Mona, guessing her intention, said quickly, "He went from here to the airport to fly to New Orleans

121

on business, Anne. Won't be back for a week. He was darned unhappy you weren't here, believe me."

"All I wanted to tell him," Anne said, "is that it isn't a crime in America to think your own thoughts, to open your own business."

A gate clanged shut across Canyon Road. Loretta Turley came self-consciously into the patio, fetching this evening in a soot-smudged blouse, levis which had been slashed off just above the knees, and thong sandals. Anne greeted her with a warm smile and told her to help herself from the available chow. Loretta filled her plate and ate greedily, as if this were her first meal that day. Almost like a somewhat irresponsible teenager, Loretta asked, "Are you mad at anyone? We all definitely have the feeling you're angry with us."

"Disappointed," Anne said; "not angry. How are you doing?"

"Well, modeling work seems hard to find just now. Everybody's doing landscapes."

"There's some lovely scenery around here to paint," Anne conceded. "I lost an hour coming home this afternoon because I noticed a mesa I'd not noticed before. It seemed to float in the air, neither earth nor sky, and its colors were beautiful, especially the soft vermilion."

Loretta gazed at the flagstones. With some hesitancy, she then said, "I could use a pad, I guess.

When I'm very rich, I'll never go back to Morales. Morales called me a lazy, shiftless girl who should be ashamed to owe so much rent and not do anything to earn the money."

Mona said promptly, "You can use my so-called room. Isn't it the dickens? A woman my age shouldn't be afraid to wake up all alone in the dark. But nothing anyone says, including my psychoanalyst, can transform me into a big brave creature. So I continue to impose on Anne's good nature, and there the room is."

Startlingly, Loretta began to cry—this young, dazzling creature who was surely the envy of most women in Santa Fe. "What's wrong with the human body?" Loretta wailed. "God made it, too. It's just as natural and beautiful as all those buttes and mesas and mountains they're painting these days!"

"If you were a little girl-child," Anne said, "I'd haul you onto my lap and comfort you. But all I can do to comfort a lovely hulk like you is to say that we like you very much and we'd feel privileged to have you stay with us for as long as you wish."

The unabashed admiration and sentiment had the desired effect. Loretta smiled happily and wiped her tears away with a corner of her blouse. She demanded to be shown her room, and Anne rose maternally and took her upstairs. Loretta tested the mattress with several vigorous bounces. She inspected her private bathroom. She gazed at the views to be seen from the three windows. "I'm not a pig," she said suddenly. "I keep myself clean and I keep my pad clean."

"Oh, we have a woman who keeps the house in order, Loretta. Mona and I work hard. We don't have much time for housework."

Inspecting the wardrobe closet, Loretta gasped. "Morales kept all my things," she complained. "Is that nice? All I have is what I'm wearing!"

Anne asked wearily, "How much do you owe?"

"Forty dollars."

Anne got the money from her handbag, and off Loretta went joyously to pay the back rent and collect her things.

Back on the patio, Mona asked Anne: "Method to your madness, darling? You're the girl who fulminated one evening about the ingratitude of these people."

"She's so darned irresponsible. I couldn't sleep, I'm sure, if I thought that maybe she was sleeping in some alley like an unwanted cat."

"Well, I can give her some clothes. It'll infuriate me to see how much more prettily she fills them than I ever did, but I'll be generous. She should get a job, though. Three's not enough work for all the women in town who think they're artists' models."

David turned into the patio from the road. He nodded when he saw them seated there, and he pulled a chair over companionably. "I thought I'd come to speak encouraging words," he said, "to a girl about to open her first art gallery."

His smile was so boyishly good-humored that Anne wondered why an unloved girl didn't grab opportunity while she could. If it was in the natural order of things for a woman to marry, and if a fellow came along into her life in the natural order of things . . . ?

"Not a bit nervous," she fibbed. "But it was sweet of you to think of me, David."

He gave her a slip of paper. The paper was a check made out to The Gallery of the Five Statues for five hundred dollars. "Parents appreciate fine gifts occasionally," he said gruffly. "Mine are celebrating a thirty-third wedding anniversary next month. I get a lot of advantage out of giving you a check like that and leaving the selection of the painting to Miss Aley. I know the painting will be worth the money."

Anne had to bite her nether lip hard to keep from crying out.

"Nice of you to remember," she finally said, "Mr. Blumberg's contention that a big sale made on opening day brings good luck to the new business forever."

Mona, the rascal, left them alone on the patio.

Chapter Thirteen

It was a warmly happy, girlishly gay Anne Hendlay who answered the wake-up call made by the paraplegic owner and operator of the .Santa Fe Rise and Shine Company. Always made uneasy by the unusual, the fellow asked, "Did I goof, Miss Hendlay, and ring later than you ordered? You sound like everybody sounds when they got some extra sleep in."

"No goof. Lovely morning, that's all."

Anne showered and powdered, put on a robe, and went downstairs to make breakfast. She supposed that she ought to feel ashamed of having let David kiss her a lingering good night at the patio gate last evening. She didn't feel anything remotely suggestive of shame, though. She felt good. Imagine there being alive in the world a young and handsome man who cared enough about you to write a fat check just to make sure you new business would be off to an auspicious start! A thought made Anne hustle to the wall telephone. After considerable ringing, she got a sleepy greeting from one David Congdon. Her invitation to come hurry-up-quick from bed to breakfast made him laugh. "Darned informal proceedings," he said. "What do you offer?"

Anne broke the connection and went back to the kitchen to make a blockbuster of a breakfast for a fellow refugee from the Blumberg retail empire. There was no time to make biscuits, she decided reluctantly, but she could and would contribute some of her mother's blueberry jam to the occasion. Ham! Eggs! Potatoes! A thick mushroom gravy to go over the eggs! And, naturally, a gallon or two of coffee!

Mona and Loretta came down the spiral staircase just as David rang the doorbell. David professed to find it very difficult indeed to breakfast with three lovely ladies who still looked pink with sleep in their housecoats. He survived the experience, however, and was chuckling with a sense of well-being when he drove Annie off in his rented car to the Indian Arts Shoppe. "I may go into business around here myself," he said. "I like this happy-go-lucky life in Santa Fe."

"What kind of business?"

"What would you suggest?"

"A variety store, probably. Perhaps you could

127

make one of those lease deals with Mr. Blumberg."

David shook his head. "I doubt he'd be receptive to any such proposition from me. Yesterday he telephoned three times. I took the last call. He's given me his final offer. Forty thousand a year."

"That," Anne said huskily, "is a lot of money."

"I imagine that's why he made the offer. An offer like that tends to make a man rethink his position on many matters."

"A man earning forty thousand a year, David, can hardly claim he's leading a conformist's life— or even the typical life of a typical corporation man. With a salary such as that, a person has it made."

But they came to the shop, and there was work for Anne to do if The Gallery of the Five Statues were to open as scheduled at eleven o'clock. Anne zipped into her own place to set things up for Nora. She put fifty dollars in the cash register drawer, she unlocked the various cases, she opened the inner shutters of the side windows. When Nora arrived, she gave the girl the news that her salary was being boosted to eighty-five dollars a week. The diminutive redhead paused in the act of putting on her emerald green smock. No smile. No little squeal of elation. Just as the silence became mutually embarrassing, Nora said thoughtfully, "I've been thinking of quitting, Miss

128

Hendlay. I guess I could stick around until the end of the month, though."

Anne didn't let it trouble her. "As you wish," she said matter-of-factly. "But for as long as you stay, you'll get the eighty-five per week."

She went on through the door that now connected the Indian Arts Shoppe and The Gallery of the Five Statues. David, bless his heart, was helping Miss Aley rearrange paintings on one of the wall. "This young man," Miss Aley explained, "thought I had too many things of one type on this wall. It didn't matter to him that the work is the work of some of the top West Coast artists. We must have variety for the sake of variety."

"I'm right, you know," David said cheerfully. "Merchandise is merchandise, regardless of the special name you give it. People like to have a selection."

They were still rearranging pictures when Mrs. Elmo Staunton and Mrs. Lund came at ten-thirty.

Anne, exercising her own judgment, led the two ladies into the gallery by way of the inter-connecting door. She allowed the lovely interior to have its effect, and then she made introductions. While Miss Aley eyed her askance, Anne said easily, "I always did appreciate professional courtesy, Mrs. Staunton. If you want to see more paintings after you've looked these over, I'll gladly take you to our storeroom."

129

Mrs. Lund said hoarsely, "That seascape is a Mrs. V. L.! I'm sure of it! I saw reproductions of her work in a Life magazine feature a few months ago."

Miss Aley smiled blandly at a young lady who'd once looked at a painting disbelievingly after four thousand dollars had been mentioned.

Anne recovered quickly and said with appropriate casualness, "Oh, yes, that's a Mrs. V. L. We have five or six of her things off in the storeroom somewhere."

She got cups and saucers and poured coffee for the ladies. Mrs. Staunton, after several sips, asked outright: "Then you don't intend to specialize in Santa Fe artists, Hendlay?"

"I suppose we intend to specialize in art, Mrs. Staunton, regardless of the subject, regardless of the region, regardless of the artist's name. Miss Aley has a fine gallery in San Francisco and connections in Chicago and New York. We may even get a Benton next week. We're negotiating for it now."

Mrs. Lund looked at Miss Aley and demanded, "What would you ask for yonder seascape? No, Catherine, don't scold me. I've always had a fondness for seascapes, and that painting is too good to pass over."

Miss Aley, Lord love her, shook her head at Mrs. Lund. "I'm the art buyer and judge here,

Mrs. Lund. Miss Hendlay manages the shop and is in charge of sales."

Eventually the hazel eyes came reluctantly to Anne's face. "Your selling price, please?" Mrs. Lund asked.

Anne promptly shook her head. "Oh, I couldn't sell it to you, Mrs. Lund," she said. "A painting like this belongs in a home or a museum; not in another art gallery."

Mrs. Staunton said firmly to Mrs. Lund, "My dear, it simply doesn't make sense, any sense at all, to support the Art Arcade and our principles and then turn around and make a purchase here. If you must have a Mrs. V. L., I'm sure the Art Arcade can find one for you."

Someone rapped on the closed patio door. Thinking it might be Mona come with a photographer to cover the grand opening, Anne unlocked the door and pulled it inward. A uniformed man stood there with a large basket of artfully arranged red roses. Mrs. Staunton said wistfully when she saw the roses, "I wish I could grow them like that. What a charming arrangement!"

Anne found the little card deep in the roses. "Good luck," it read. There was no signature, but one wasn't necessary. Anne turned back to the mother of the man who'd sent the roses. "I do have to dispute something Mrs. Staunton has said, Mrs. Lund. Miss Aley is the exclusive agent for

Mrs. V. L. paintings. The Art Arcade may find other things for you, but not a Mrs. V. L. painting."

Mrs. Lund said crisply, "What are you asking for the painting? You've not answered my question."

Figuring she had nothing to lose, Anne said easily, "Six thousand dollars, Mrs. Lund."

Anne fancied she heard Miss Aley sigh behind her.

Anne took the seascape from the wall and carried it across the gallery to one of the empty panels. She flicked on a ceiling light and set a chair before the painting. "You're certainly welcome to sit here and study it," she invited Mrs. Lund. "Or, if you'd prefer, I could have the painting hung in your home for a week or so. No charge, of course. We'd consider it a privilege."

Spoken softly, with just a touch of deference, the offer had an agreeable effect upon Mrs. Lund. She gave thought to the proposal, her brows drawn together as Robert sometimes drew his. She said presently to Mrs. Staunton, "I see no principle involved here. The work is uncontestably art, and certainly the subject is in all respects acceptable.

"Still! My husband has strong views on the subject of business procedures, and he distinctly told me that if we're to operate a successful art center, we must give no aid or comfort to our competition."

Mrs. Lund turned to Anne, rising. "You may send the painting tomorrow afternoon," she announced. "Do you wish me to sign a paper or something?"

"Oh, that wouldn't be necessary, Mrs. Lund."

Mrs. Staunton was still expostulating when the ladies left. In the gallery, no one said a word until the ladies had gone out through the patio gate, and then Miss Aley turned to Anne and nodded approval. "That was exactly the right tone to take," she said, "I think you asked too much, however. A well-run gallery has many repeat customers. The customers buy again and again because they have confidence in the dealer. Generally speaking, it's relatively easy to overcharge anyone once. But you don't develop a clientele that way."

Anne chuckled. "I just couldn't resist making Mrs. Staunton's eyes pop, Miss Aley."

"Give her an hour or so to get home and then telephone Mrs. Lund that you made a mistake. Tell her that you've checked your books and discovered that the asking price on this painting is four thousand."

David, Anne noticed, was looking at the card that had come with the roses. Amused, she went on to the door and opened it wide to the sunlight and warmth of the June day. She stood smiling and greeting the men and women who came in from the patio. While the crowd wasn't as large as she'd hoped it would be, it was a good turn-out of well dressed people who'd obviously come to look at paintings rather than just attend an advertised event. David, the Blumberg-trained rascal, waited for a lull in the conversation and then asked Miss Aley loudly when he could expect delivery of his painting. "When I pay five hundred for something," he said, "I like to get possession in a hurry."

Miss Aley assured him sweetly that he could have possession by tomorrow morning at the latest. Miss Aley got a SOLD tag from the desk at the rear and taped it to an Elice Popham painting of golden aspens growing in a rugged mountain setting complete with mountain creek and several jagged peaks. There was a general murmur, and people went over to study the painting. Anne saw to it that everyone was served coffee and cake and then, not sure she wouldn't giggle if she watched David in action much longer, she returned to her own shop to see how Nora was getting along.

Still cool, Nora reported, "I've sold a flock of Chimayo table scarves, Miss Hendlay. We're getting pretty low on them, too."

"I'll order more. Care to pop over to the gallery for a while? Frankly, I prefer the work of our Santa Fe artists, but Miss Aley tells me that many of our paintings over there are rather good. Mr. Congdon has bought an Elice Popham landscape for five hundred dollars, and Mrs. Lund is interested in a Mrs. V. L. seascape that costs four thousand."

Nora said tautly, "And everybody else can starve, is that it?"

Unsurprised, Anne sat behind her desk. "I wondered when something like that would be said," she told Nora. "I don't think that anyone *not* an art dealer has done more for the young artists we know than I. Sunday afternoon entertainment and chow, a place to show their things. And most of the time I never even charged a commission. So, of course, I'm the scoundrel. I actually risked my neck to display Tom's statues, but that means nothing, either."

"For your information," Nora said heatedly, "the Art Arcade won't give advances now that they know you won't."

Anne telephoned Mrs. Lund and reported the so-called error she'd found. Mrs. Lund gave a pleased laugh. "I *did* think the price a bit high," she said, "which is why I didn't buy the picture promptly. In this case—well, you may consider the picture bought."

Anne waited hopefully for more, the important more, but Mrs. Lund just hung up softly.

Chapter Fourteen

By the middle of July it became apparent even to Anne that The Gallery of the Five Statues would establish itself solidly in the cultural life of old Santa Fe and be a fine source of income for as long as it remained in business. It became apparent to her, also, that Mr. David Congdon was of two minds about this big and important turn in her affairs. He was clearly pleased for her, but he was clearly displeased by the demands that the new enterprise made upon her time. One Saturday morning he asked, "Where's all this easy living Santa Fe is supposed to provide? What with running two shops and buying for Blumberg, you're as busy as a motor on a twenty-four-hour assembly line."

Dressed in a striped tan and white searsucker suit, wearing a wide-brimmed straw to protect her face from the sun, Anne got behind the wheel of her spanking new Ford station wagon. "You mustn't ever scold a girl," she chided. "Especially, you must never scold a girl when she's wearing a new suit and a new hat and driving a new car for the first time."

David looked at the dashboard. "You should've bought an air-conditioner. I never knew a high mountain area could be so hot."

"I love heat," Anne confessed. "When I look back at my girlhood in Idaho, I wonder if I was ever truly warm. I'm sure I was. Mothers do hug their little girl infants snuggle-tight. But I never remember being entirely warm."

"Where do we go today?" David asked.

Anne's pleasure in her new car and her clothes and her cleverness went winging. She said slowly, a trifle nervously, "Well, I tricked you, David, when I told you to pack enough things for a three-day tour of Indian country. We're going—well, I thought we'd drive to Denver."

His jaw muscles tightened. Briefly, his eyes flashed.

Anne said insistently, "You're very nice, David. If you really want to live and perhaps work in Santa Fe, I'll be glad. But sooner or later play has to end. At your age, you're too young and poor to retire."

"How much is Mr. Blumberg paying you to deliver me to Denver? Has he promised to give you another fifty thousand or so to spend on handicrafts?"

Hurt, Anne muttered, "That's nasty, David."

"Well, what am I to think? What difference should it make to you if I choose to stay out of the Blumberg rat race?"

"Simple," Anne said. "I had a thirty-minute telephone conversation with Mr. Blumberg on Monday. You have until the end of the month, at the latest, to come to terms with him. After that, he'll just have to put someone else in charge of the Wyoming expansion. He can't delay any longer. And if he does have to put someone else in charge, you won't ever have any kind of future with him."

"I knew that when I resigned."

Anne asked, "Did you really, David? I don't think you knew any such thing. Stupid men never climb so high or so fast as you climbed in the Blumberg organization. I think you knew when you resigned that Mr. Blumberg would come after you. I think you even knew that he'd raise his original offer."

Easily, not making a big show of it, Anne started the new car.

"You're very beautiful," David said, "in your new summer dress. You're much more beautiful in your new summer dress than Beulah Cummings was yesterday."

A queer little chill settled around Anne's heart.

138

Somehow she managed to keep the car moving in a straight line along the road, and somehow she managed to say in a flat tone of voice, "You can't ever compare apples and oranges, so you can't ever compare this girl's beauty with that girl's beauty. Each girl is an individual. Therefore, each girl is as different as an apple is different from an orange. We may be fruit, but we're different kinds of fruit."

"A knock sounded on my door, I thought it was you, and there was Beulah."

And yet, Anne thought with satisfaction, he had dutifully packed a bag to come with her so that she could show him more country while she made a three-day buying trip.

David looked at her levelly for a minute, and then his manner underwent a change. "We'll go to Denver if you want to," he said. "It will be a waste of time, but we'll go."

They reached Denver around sunset, and Anne was tired after the long drive along mountain roads and still upset because of the narrow road she'd had to take between Silverton and Ouray, a road that wound along a gorge so deep and wild it had made her dizzy to look at it. They each took rooms at the Brown Palace, and they dined in Elitch's Gardens. Anne telephoned Mr. Blumberg that they were in town, and Debbie was waiting in the hotel lobby when they returned late from high adventure in the amusement area of the Gardens. Debbie was now a slim, sophisticated young woman. She wore a simple black dress, gloves, a discreet string of pearls. "How delightful to see you again," Debbie said with unexpected formality. "I do hope you are prospering in Santa Fe."

Anne kissed her anyway, and Debbie stopped being sophisticated just long enough to give her an emotional hug. "Dad said I can ride back with you for the final flaunting of summer," Debbie announced. "Do you still entertain all those ridiculous artists?"

Anne finally got an opportunity to introduce David. Debbie looked him over coolly. "I'm not sure I want to know you," she reported. "You've been an irritant to my Dad's peace of mind."

David said amusedly, "Oh, I'm not a bad fellow, Miss Blumberg. I just have my own philosophy, that's all."

"And what's that?" Debbie asked challengingly. "I'm majoring in philosophy, it so happens."

"Just that girls in their summer dresses are at least as important in life as a Blumberg Variety Store."

Debbie gave Anne a pitying look. "You do find the nuts, don't you?" she asked.

Debbie spent the night with Anne. She shed her sophistication with her clothes. "Will I have the same room that I had last year?" she asked. "I adored that room. I always woke up early so that I'd hear the clip-clop of the burro's hoofs in the alley. What a quaint way to deliver the morning milk!"

Anne gave her a nightie to put on. Debbie stood admiring herself in the bureau mirror. "Are you sweet on David Congdon?" she asked. "He has a special way of looking at you."

"Whoa. Some things a girl doesn't tell even her best friend!"

"It's nice to be sweet on a boy," Debbie said softly. She swung around, actually blushing. "I'm sweet on a boy. You wouldn't believe anyone could be sweet on Louis, not really. He's short and pretty fat, and he's centuries older than I, and I dare say you'd call him a type of oaf. Every time he comes to the house for dinner, my parents positively shudder. I guess Louis has just one dress-up suit, and that's rather antique."

"But?"

Debbie got into bed beside Anne, and Anne switched off the lamp. They had a room that was situated in exactly the right position to be lighted intermittently by the reds and greens of a fluorescent sign across the road. Debbie asked suddenly, "Is Mona still afraid of the dark?"

"Yes. Oh, and that reminds me, Debbie. We have another girl living with us now. Remember Loretta Turley, that lovely model?"

141

"That tremendous Nordic in the sloppy-Joe outfit?"

"Well, she's having a difficult time, I'm afraid. The point is, you'll have to share her room. We never did get around to furnishing the third bedroom."

"It's all right. We'll talk about men, about Louis. Have I told you he's a doctor—a general practitioner? It's very interesting. There's a lot of anti-Semitism where Louis practices, but he has more work than he should be doing. Everybody tells him that for a Jew he's all right."

"People are that way, I suppose. I'm all right in my way for Robert Lund, for example, and I may even be worthy of marrying him should I allow Mrs. Lund to smooth out my rough edges."

Debbie giggled. "Louis is just as bad in his way, though," she said. "He tells me that his clients aren't so bad, considering most of them are Gentiles. Anyway, poor Dad doesn't know what to do about me. He attributes my interest in Louis, a non-businessman yet, to my faulty education. Dad thinks that the more you study philosophy, which is really a study of life, the more confused you become about life."

"Could be that your father is right."

Debbie prattled on about her Louis, and she was still prattling when Anne fell asleep. Debbie became quite a sophisticated young woman again, however, when she put on her clothes in the morning. "I'll dash home and pack," she said, "while you're having your little business chat with Dad. Walk softly! Dad's all tension these days, the poor dear, about that expansion into Wyoming. Is your David Congdon really that competent?"

"I don't think he's my David Congdon," Anne said. "I may never marry, come to think of it. I may just make hundreds of millions of dollars."

Yet she was nervous, and for David Congdon, when they went into Mr. Blumberg's office Sunday morning at eleven. Entering the suite evoked memories of Blumberg tantrums she'd witnessed more than once when she's sat at yonder desk. She covered up her nervousness with a smile as Mr. Blumberg reared up to greet them and wave them to chairs. Mr. Blumberg told her politely that she didn't look a day older, and then he swung to David Congdon. "Young fellow," he rumbled, "I don't know if you're worth bothering with any more. What kind of one-cylinder brain do you have? So you've got a few pennies in the bank! Big deal! All of a sudden you're too rich to make a real future for yourself and your life and your family? You must be a nut. Do you know what it costs to educate just one child these days? I'll show you my daughter's bills."

At that point, Anne stopped feeling nervous. When Mr. Blumberg talked in terms of family, he wasn't preparing to pull a mental gun out of its holster to shoot anyone dead.

"I needed to get away," David Congdon explained. "Suddenly I saw the creature I was becoming—the corporation man with a big future and nothing else. Girls in their summer dresses were making fellows happy . . . and I was always walking alone."

"Beulah Cummings? Gorgeous girl. Fine catch!"

David's eyes seemed to become stones suddenly.

Mr. Blumberg nodded. "All right," he said. "I won't push that if you don't want me to. I'll talk business. Fifty thousand a year. If it kills you to dress and live as I want my executives to do, suit yourself. And that's it, Congdon. Take it or leave it."

David looked at Anne. "Marry me?" David asked.

Somehow, Anne managed not to say a word, not a single word.

David pursed his lips. After a time, he looked at Mr. Blumberg and said, "I accept your offer, sir."

Chapter Fifteen

Throughout the return trip to Santa Fe, Debbie Blumberg and David Congdon did most of the talking. Debbie told David that the phrase, "girls in their summer dresses," reminded her of a lovely book of that title which had been written by her favorite contemporary writer, Mr. Irwin Shaw. Then, with a wisdom far beyond her years, Debbie said maternally to David, "But you won't get very far in life, I think, by thinking of women as lovely, lovely goodies to want because you've never had any. Truly, I grow so weary of innocent people who are just dying to have experience. To be is to experience. Anyway, there are many unhappy men walking with girls in summer dresses."

Anne dropped David off at the entrance to La Posada. He asked in a pained tone of voice when he would see her. "We have a lot to discuss," he said miserably. "Back there at the office—you misunderstood."

145

After they'd driven on, Debbie said gigglingly, "You must teach me to torment Louis that way. Men are strange. They want everything on their own terms!"

"You'll not say anything to Mona or Loretta about any of this, will you?"

"Oh, dear. I hate people who make you make promises. But it's a go. Whee, I'm back in Santa Fe!"

There was a kissing reunion in the living room, with Mona hugging the young lady and Debbie joyfully swatting Mona's rump. Young scholar and young model measured one another carefully and apparently decided they liked one another. With pretty grace, Loretta picked up one of Debbie's suitcases and led the girl up the spiral staircase. When they'd gone, Anne felt as if she'd gotten away from a storm at last. "Debbie packs a lot of energy," she told Mona ruefully. "You missed a lively debate about life and other things today."

Mona went to the couch and sat down, crossed her legs and smiled. "Speaking of other things?" she prompted.

"Mr. Blumberg offered David fifty thousand a year, and David accepted. Later, Mr. Blumberg telephoned me that the Indian handicrafts are doing well and that he'll put his ordering on a regular basis—ten thousand a month. Five percent of a hundred and twenty thousand a year comes to six thousand a year, or five hundred a month. That's practically net income, because I make buying trips anyway."

Mona was impressed. "You have a way of turning things to your advantage, haven't you?" she asked. "I remember back in April how scared you were about those statues, you attracted Miss Aley's attention—and there's an art gallery."

"A great deal of luck," Anne said firmly.

"What's your monthly income, Anne? I know its way up there. The new car . . . loads of new clothes . . . the respectful way the manager greets you when we sometimes go into the bank."

"Right now," Anne said simply, "about twenty-five thousand a year."

All the softness drained from Mona's face. "A substantial income," she said huskily. "I may be raised to eight thousand a year next year."

Anne bit her lip.

Mona closed her eyes and sighed. She shook her head. "Oh, it's all right," she said gently. "I won't resent your success. It all amounts to doing what you want to do with your life. I always wanted to write on art."

The next moment, without intending to, Anne told her about David's proposal in Mr. Blumberg's office. "I just couldn't answer," she said, puzzled. "I was choked up with all sorts of emotions. But

147

most of all, I didn't want to abandon all this. Not for him. Isn't he a strange man, a pathetic man?"

Anne put the proposal out of her mind. Although it was late, she got into her new station wagon again and drove to the shop. She unlocked the patio gate and went swiftly, eagerly to the gallery first, because the lights were still on and she could see Miss Aley at the desk in the rear. Miss Aley glanced up quickly as she came in. "Ah," she said, "the wanderer has returned. Nice trip?"

"Nice."

"Eventful?"

"What's eventful?"

"This was an eventful day here," Miss Aley said. "Around three o'clock a delegation of young artists came here looking for you. They were led by that skinny sculptor with the greasy blond hair —Tom Zimmerman. They were disappointed that you weren't here."

Anne sat on a corner of the desk, guessing the rest.

"They've become disenchanted with the Art Arcade," Miss Aley said. "No advances, and very few sales. I like to conduct business in an ethical manner, so I told those young people they should be patient with Mrs. Staunton and the others. But they'd like to make an arrangement with us."

And some work would be good and other work

would be less good, Anne reflected. But even the good wouldn't be especially good, for these were young men and women who had much to learn about techniques, color, composition, and even concepts. In the past she'd been able to sell occasional things for them, but only at low prices and only after months and months of displaying the work.

"I think not," she told Miss Aley. "During this boycott by them, I've had a chance to think about them and their work. They talk fine art, and they're lively people to have around. But they're not ready yet, do you think?"

"Tom Zimmerman, possibly. And perhaps Ellen Roninger. Miss Roninger's abstracts are peculiarly and charmingly appealing. I'm glad you feel about this as I feel. I'll take Tom and Ellen, though."

Nodding, feeling sad about all the others, Anne went through the connecting door to the Indian Arts Shoppe. To her surprise, a light was burning in the storage room. She investigated and found Nora O'Dell doing some sort of inventory work. She remembered then that Nora planned to leave once the inventory had been completed. "I'm sorry you dislike me so much," she joked, "that you'll work on your own time to complete that inventory."

"I just think I'll be happier elsewhere, Miss

Hendlay. You've changed so much. You used to have some feeling for people, some understanding of people. When you stuck up for Tom's statues while everyone was calling them obscene—well, in a way I loved you. But just because Peter Underwood came swaggering along one night, and just because all the artists let dreams of money go to their heads . . . well, you've changed."

"A ruthless career girl walking to success over the bodies of the starving poor, is that it?"

"You could've been more understanding!"

"Perhaps. And then again, perhaps not."

"No wonder Robert Lund dropped you! The moment you saw a chance to grab more money, you went out and grabbed."

Anne thought to herself that she didn't have to take abuse from this redheaded snip or from anyone else.

"And how sweet of you to offer me a whole eighty-five a week, Miss Hendlay, when you're making fifteen thousand a year from this business alone!"

Anne half turned to the door. "Well, if that's how you feel, Nora," she said quietly, "I think you're wise to leave. Don't bother about the inventory. Let me write a check for the salary due you and for a month's vacation. I never write letters of recommendation, but if you'll have prospective

150

employers telephone me, I'll give you a top recommendation."

"I don't need one," Nora said haughtily. "I was offered a hundred a week by Mrs. Staunton. I could've left long before this. I could've had dates with David Congdon, too. But I was loyal. Isn't that funny?"

Anne felt herself pale. "David asked you for dates?"

"And a lot of other girls, too—all so sweet and pretty in their summer dresses! Mona Yates and Loretta Turley and a lot of hungry female artists and—"

Nora O'Dell stopped talking, staring at Anne's face as if at some horror. It seemed to Anne that an eternity went by, at the very least, and then Nora started to cry very softly and nervously. "I don't want to leave," she cried. "We always got along."

Anne thought that if one more tear were shed, she'd scream. She got a hankie from her handbag and dried the girl's eyes roughly. "It was your idea to leave," she snapped; "not mine. And you're wrong about many other things, but this isn't the place to discuss them. Go pretty your face and I'll buy you dinner."

Nora did her best, but she wasn't the loveliest woman in the world to look at when she came out of the lavatory in her inexpensive, poorly styled suit. Anne took her to the Three Cities of Spain, her favorite restaurant in Santa Fe, because the food was always superb and the place delightfully informal.

"Whatever I said," Nora said there, "was a lie."

Anne said crisply, "We plan to take work from Tom Zimmerman and Ellen Roninger. The others aren't ready for a big-time gallery yet. I'm sure, however, that Miss Aley won't mind if we put the work of some of the other artists in our shop, as of old. As for your future: no one runs until he can walk. You came to me a couple of years ago fresh out of high school. Your present raise is the fourth raise you've had in two years. I'm finding it possible to leave you alone in the shop now. In another year or so you'll be qualified to manage the shop. I can't promise you a thousand a month, because my business won't ever become a whopper like that. But you could reach a hundred and fifty a week in another year or so. And if business improves, you could reach more."

Nora said shakily, "I have to earn for Tom, you see. We're being married."

Anne asked: "When?"

"Well, he does have to earn something a week. He does understand that."

Anne came close to asking: "Couldn't you have told me that?" But it all seemed so unimportant to her now. After long thought, she said, "I can't

152

match Mrs. Staunton's offer, Nora. I run a business. I don't have her capital. If you think the Art Arcade is there to stay and you need the extra money, you'd be foolish to remain with me."

"I'll just have to think about it, Miss Hendlay."

Anne put her in a taxi after dinner, and then she drove on up Canyon Road to her home. Mona was alone in the living room, watching television. She met Anne's grave brown eyes, and suddenly she flushed and turned off the set. "All right," she said. "I should be doing something more constructive than watching such programs."

Anne asked, puzzled: "How come David, Mona? I mean, on the sneak? I never complained one evening when he sat there giving you the full treatment."

"A woman likes to eat dinner, to dance, to hear silly words in the moonlight. It stopped, believe me, when I noticed you becoming more interested in him."

"That man!"

"Well," Mona Yates consoled her, "if there are a lot of headaches in that man, there's fun in him, too."

Chapter Sixteen

Looking tanned and handsome, and trying to seem casual, too, Robert Lund came back into Anne's life on the afternoon of August sixth. She knew the date because she was at her desk at the time, writing checks. A throat was cleared, she glanced up, and there he stood. He was wearing an Italian silk suit that hung and draped beautifully.

"I thought we might have dinner together," Robert said firmly. "I know it's short notice, but there you are."

Anne felt as if there were a commotion in her chest. For three or four seconds, breathing was oddly difficult. Then she was herself, and she heard her cool voice saying, "I'm afraid I'm booked, Robert. Have you ever met David Congdon? This is a going-away dinner. He's to establish umpteen Blumberg Variety Stores in Wyoming."

"I've heard of him," Robert said sarcastically. "You'd be astonished if you knew how many people have told me about you two."

"Well," Anne said politely, "it was nice of you to think of me."

Mrs. Lund came several afternoons later, presumably to look at the paintings in the gallery. Anne told her pleasantly that Miss Aley would be glad to show her some new paintings which had just been received, and at this point Mrs. Lund sat on the chair beside the desk and gazed about at the various Indian handicrafts. "I understand you've lost the services of Miss O'Dell," she said. "I was a bit unhappy when Mrs. Staunton telephoned me about it. I'm always made uneasy when people steal servants or staff from one another."

"Nora needed more salary than I could give her, Mrs. Lund. I was sorry to lose her, but I understood."

"Now you have no one?"

"Well, I've been interviewing, of course. It would have to be a girl younger than I. I could never quite bring myself to the point of ordering an older woman around as an employer sometimes does have to order. My mother raised me to respect my elders, I'll tell you that!"

Without any preliminary throat-clearing, Mrs.

Lund said softly, "Robert and I have been quarreling about you."

"Oh, I'm sorry to hear that."

"Robert apparently blames me for a certain unhappiness this spring and summer. I was quite surprised, as was my sister, when he blurted that out at table."

Anne almost pitied her. And then she wondered why in the world she should pity Mrs. Lund. The woman had serenely gone her way as if only her happiness, her idea of the fitness of things, were to be considered. It wasn't even as if Robert had become interested in a nobody. Any person who worked honestly at any job was a great big somebody!

"I'm very busy," Anne said hopefully. "I must do my books between customers now."

"You mustn't hate me, you know."

"I don't," Anne said carefully. She realized with a start of pleasure that she didn't even dislike Mrs. Lund. She closed the book she'd been checking and switched the desk lamp off. "All it ever amounts to, it seems to me," she said, "is that a mother wants the best for her son, and that's perfectly natural, perfectly right. The girl who's being appraised by the mother naturally thinks of herself as being the best girl for him, perhaps even the only girl for him. So there's a clash of some kind or another unless the mother and the girl establish a rapport almost the moment they meet. A girl of my experience—well, she learns to be objective about clashes of any kind. In an executive suite or in a shop, she soon learns that even violent differences of opinion are perfectly normal."

"I do try to be fair," Mrs. Lund said in a defensive tone. "That I came here and bought a painting despite Mrs. Staunton's objections proves that I try to be fair."

The defensive tone interested Anne. She studied the woman more closely, admiring her loveliness and erect posture. About the well-formed mouth she saw the little lines made by muscles in tension. The nostrils had a faintly pinched appearance: another indication of tension. Most revelatory of all were the hazel eyes. In their expression was a quality of uncertainty. Anne knew positively in that moment that somehow she'd achieved a kind of dominance over Mrs. Lund, and for two or three seconds she felt exhilarated by the knowledge. Then she was herself again. Dominance over any human being, she thought, was the last thing in the world she wanted. It was quite enough in life to make one's way, to develop emotionally and intellectually, to enjoy one's friends, to do work that was interesting and rewarding. Let Robert be the person to fire a creature because she had a wart on her nose. Let David be the person to buy a dream in the form of a girl in summer dress.

Let the poor young artists be the persons to try to back an old friend into a business corner. to dominate in the various naked and subtle ways open to a person, you had to hurt. Let others do the hurting. . . .

"Yes, I was fair," Mrs. Lund said insistently, obviously troubled by Anne's failure to agree with her. "I never told Robert that I wouldn't accept you. On the contrary! I offered to do more for you than I've ever offered to do for anyone else."

"What's the problem?" Anne asked kindly. "You look disturbed."

"He's left our home. He was a different man when he returned from that business trip to New Orleans. I scarcely knew him. Oh, he was polite and gentle; he always is. He simply informed me that in New Orleans he'd walked for hours in Jackson Square, thinking about the pattern of his life. He informed me that he'd decided to lead a life closer to his idea of what life ought to be. We talked. I couldn't dissuade him from his decision to take his own apartment, even to run his business as he thinks he wants to run it now."

Anne's fingers began to tingle. She relaxed the set of her arms across her chest.

"He blamed me," Mrs. Lund said bleakly, "for your strained relations."

Miss Aley came through the connecting door, Mrs. Staunton beside her. Mrs. Staunton looked surprised when she saw Mrs. Lund at the desk. "No wonder I couldn't get you on the telephone, dear," she said to Mrs. Lund. "How lucky that you're here! We had a simply dreadful meeting of the Plateau Club's board of directors this morning. Several girls took the position that it's utter madness to continue to operate a gallery that attracts so little interest. One girl reported on a very clever investigation she'd made of our sales to date. All the sales, will you believe it, were made to members of the Plateau Club! Truly, I was shocked. I agreed entirely with her that it's preposterous to operate a gallery so that we may buy paintings from it. It would certainly be less expensive if we bought the paintings from a gallery whose overhead we didn't have to assume. Don't you agree?"

"Our objectives were different, Mrs. Staunton. As I understood it, we were interested primarily in elevating the standards of these young artists."

"And they should be elevated, no question of that. Nudity! Grotesquerie! Abstracts so abstract that not even the artists can explain them! But the girls thought we could make our influence felt in a less costly way. And Miss Aley has made a fascinating proposal along those lines. Miss Aley has proposed that the Plateau Club establish three awards annually for local young artists between eighteen and thirty-five. We would award a thousand dollars each for the finest work in oil, water color, and sculpture."

Anne's eyes shone. "Why, that's a grand idea!" she told Miss Aley.

"Naturally," Mrs. Staunton said, "the selection committee of the Plateau Club would be influenced in its decision by the nature of the subject matter. Those disgusting statues out in the patio, for example, would hardly qualify Mr. Zimmerman for an award."

Wisely, Anne didn't argue. The important thing was to get the awards established. Later in the game, next year, say, she could establish a similar award for practitioners of other than so-called moral and representational art.

"Anyway," Mrs. Staunton informed Mrs. Lund, "the board of directors has voted to close the Art Arcade. After consultation with my husband, I have decided to purchase the Art Arcade from the Plateau Club for a price that will compensate our treasurer for all the expenses incurred. It appears that I require another tax deduction, of all things!"

Anne shot a glance at Miss Aley, who smiled faintly.

"Mrs. Staunton thought it would be nice," Miss Aley said, "if we lent professional direction to this expansion of her salon. We would choose for exhibition in her new establishment the best of the work these young Santa Fe artists are doing—subject to certain conditions, of course. We would handle all sales, and the commission from these, plus a small fee, would be our compensation."

Anne asked quickly, "What about Nora O'Dell, Mrs. Staunton?"

"You may have her back," Mrs. Staunton said graciously. "I don't need to pay anyone a hundred dollars a week to open the doors each day and just sit around to make certain there's no theft or vandalism."

Anne turned back to Mrs. Lund. "It would appear," she said, "that I'm to become more deeply involved than ever in crass business. You should know, I think, that I'm not at all unhappy about it. We people who work—we get things done, and things need to be done in any society, be it monarchistic, democratic, or communistic. I suppose you could say that I'm contentedly living the life I want to live."

Mrs. Staunton looked puzzled. Then her laugh signified that she understood. "My dear girl," she told Mrs. Lund, "you must stop interfering with the course of true love. Now I have the right to say that, for you yourself asked me to take Hendlay in tow and make something of her. But Hendlay is a something! No less a personage than my husband has said so—and he's very clever about such things. It was my husband who sent me here to

161

make these arrangements. Would he have done so had he not respected Hendlay as a something?"

Mrs. Lund, her control magnificent under the circumstances. "It would please me," she said softly, "if you would dine with my family on Sunday next, at five o'clock."

Nor did Mrs. Lund press for an answer. She nodded to them and took Mrs. Elmo Staunton by the arm and left.

Miss Aley chuckled. "Nice ladies," she commented. "It isn't the world they think it is, but they're nice. I'm pleased that Nora is coming back. I want to go to San Francisco soon and dispose of my gallery. I think we're going to have a very nice operation here."

"And if I decide which love to hold?" Anne challenged.

"Even a wife and mother can find time to supervise the operation of a business, I'm sure."

Anne nodded. Even if she did become a wife and mother, she thought, she'd darned well find the time!

Chapter Seventeen

On Sunday morning, Miss Debbie Blumberg suggested that levis and a sweat shirt would be just the thing for Anne to wear to Mrs. Lund's dinner. Debbie made the suggestion while sitting Turkish fashion at the foot of Anne's bed, her dark eyes flashing wickedly, her young body quivering with sophomoric glee. "It's very important philosophically," Debbie explained, "to establish your own identity in your own mind. Only after you've become a person to yourself are you qualified to make your first awkward probings into philosophy."

"A girl should have friend husband," Anne said. "There's my philosophy."

"Deep down under that business veneer, you're a gooey person, did you know?"

Loretta came in with that lithe grace that always made Anne think of a panther. Loretta was wearing baby doll nightwear which Debbie had bought for her. Loretta gave Debbie a buddy-buddy push and squeezed onto the bed beside her. Anne looked them over fondly and chuckled. "Kids," she said, "I adore you, too. But this bed wasn't built to accommodate tons."

Debbie glanced at Loretta, and Loretta nodded. "Well," Debbie said, "we have something to tell you. In a nutshell, irrationality has returned to Santa Fe. Women in their autumn dresses aren't girls in their summer dresses, but irrationality has returned.

Anne sat up slowly, unbelievingly.

"He must love you deeply," Debbie said. "Not many men just stroll away from fifty thousand a year and a bright business future."

Anne Hendlay whispered incredulously, "I don't believe it."

"You were sleeping when he called at three this morning," Loretta said. "I took the message. He wants to have dinner with you. I told him sure."

"On my advice," Debbie said. "I'm sure Dad would disown me if he heard me, but as I've always said to my Louis, money isn't everything."

Anne scrambled out of bed. "The man's crazy! Girls in their summer dresses! He must've dated all the girls in town, judging from the reports I've gotten!"

But she was laughing foolishly as she spoke,

164

and then she pattered excitedly to her dresser and pulled out lingerie and stockings. "You help Mona run this afternoon's salon," she told Loretta. "You may as well tell everyone that you're my assistant at the Indian Arts Shoppe and the gallery. Same terms as always, but you can stress to the boys and girls that we'll now be in a better position than ever to sell their things."

Loretta sat looking stunned for a moment. Anne told her fondly that people who worked for her didn't just sit around saying thanks. Anne said that people who worked for her at least had the decency to get breakfast together for an employer who'd have a darned busy day. Loretta and Debbie finally went down to prepare breakfast, and Anne promptly went to the bedside telephone and rang Mr. David Congdon at La Posada. He answered in a cute drowsy voice but woke up in a hurry when he recognized her voice. "My last moments with Mr. Blumberg," he said, "weren't peaceful. Not ever again, not in all my life, will I be a Blumberg corporation man."

"I see."

"He doesn't blame you. You did the job you said you'd do. You got me to his office in Denver. He said he admired you that day, because you obviously didn't want to get me within earshot of a fantastic offer. I'd guess that you'll buy Indian handicrafts for him for many years to come."

"Come over for breakfast," Anne urged. "I can show you some Indian country, if you like. But I do have an important dinner date."

"Date?"

"A man wants to marry me," Anne said directly. "A very fine, upstanding, respected member of the community."

"You're now worthy of Robert Lund?"

Anne pronged the handset gently, smilingly. She went downstairs and told the kitchen crew that an unemployed male was coming for breakfast. She joined Mona out in the patio. Mona was putting cracked corn into a metal-work bird feeder. Mona said, "Fred Vicks brought this over yesterday. It's a peace offering, darling. Fred explained that he had to think of his family first. Fred said that wives and children do have to eat."

"Oh, I understood that, Mona. I was unhappy about his decision, but I knew the reason behind it. Do you know that David's back? Not ever again, not in all his life, will he be a Blumberg corporation man."

"I know."

"It's strange, Mona. I could understand a Tom Zimmerman doing that. Artists at least have the courage of their convictions. But David never seemed the type."

"Maybe up there in Wyoming, the girls never wear summer dresses."

166

Anne asked nervously, "Good heavens, what do I tell him?"

"That you'll marry him."

"Certainly! The sensible thing to do! Know a man just a handful of weeks, get hopping mad at him, but marry him anyway! Only I'm not the type. I'm the type of person who plans very carefully and builds up a business in accordance with that plan."

"Tush! The gallery fell into your lap. The arrangement with Mrs. Staunton fell into your lap because the gallery fell into your lap. I'll admit that you did develop the Indian Arts Shoppe according to plan, but that's all you did. Even the buying arrangement with Mr. Blumberg fell into your lap, because David was in Santa Fe and he wanted you to get David to Denver."

"And Robert?"

Mona stood quietly for a long time, looking not at Anne but up at the royal blue New Mexico sky. "Well," Mona said, "I don't imagine you'll have to do anything about Robert if you don't want to. I took the liberty of telephoning Mrs. Lund you'd not be coming to dinner. Mrs. Lund asked why not. I said there's a man around to whom you're worth more than fifty thousand a year, even though he never had the chance Robert had to appraise your truth worth."

"If you said that—" Anne began, and stopped.

167

Very conscious that she'd also been worth a five-hundred-dollar check back in June, she flushed and sat on one of the metal patio chairs. Some sparrows rustled to landings on the bird feeder. A truck came along the road very slowly, the driver tossing newspapers from the cab to the different patios and front yards. The plopping of their newspaper on to the flagstones frightened the birds away. Mona picked the paper up and said not without pride, "I have a good article in this one. I've announced the annual awards to be given by the Plateau Club. In my elaboration, I did some very sincere writing. I said, among other things, that Santa Fe is fortunate to have such art-minded women among its citizens."

"We are, you know. That's why I never took pot shots at them or even tried to compete with them. I thought they were wrong, I thought that the Art Arcade wouldn't last, but I never took pot shots or competed."

A cab turned into Canyon Road. Anne and Mona stood there side by side at the patio gate, and Mona said, "We've been through a lot together, you and I. You were a scared business wheel in the making, and I was a scared art writer struggling for a foothold. I'm awfully glad that it's ending like this."

"Ending?"

"I have an offer from a newspaper in New

York. Society page stuff, with emphasis upon the cultural activities of the so-called Four Hundred. I'm to get ninety-five hundred a year and a by-line."

"Really?"

"All my life," Mona said huskily, "I've dreamed of being a reporter in New York. So few ever make it. You'd be astonished if you knew how fierce the competition is."

"But I don't want you to leave!"

Mona just laughed as if at a foolish girl-child and turned away from the gate as the cab approached. David got out with some degree of nonchalance and paid the driver. He smiled at Anne. "You wouldn't like Wyoming," he said. "The land is beautiful, and the people are warm and friendly. But they don't have this mellow sun, and they don't have this charming city."

"Hi," Anne said easily. "I think you're a fool, David Congdon."

He came into the patio and pushed her elbows close to her body and then kissed her forehead. "I'm never a fool," he contradicted. "This is the only life on earth I'll ever have. I can't believe I was born only for the purpose of fretting about the well being of the Blumberg corporation."

"And what do you plan to do?"

"Savor the romantic life in old Santa Fe in enchanted New Mexico. After breakfast, for exam-

169

ple, I plan to walk hand in hand with a girl along the ancient streets of the old quarter. I want to look at a plaza that was old before this nation was even born. I want to sit on a bench in that plaza with a girl and think long thoughts about the way her face looked one day when I asked her to marry me."

"I thought you were making that a condition of your acceptance of the offer, you see."

"No."

"Yes."

"We won't ever fib to one another," David said, "nor to ourselves. You couldn't give up all this, could you? That was your first thought that day, and you never got beyond that. Mr. Blumberg knew. The last time I saw him, he wasn't a business tycoon at all. He was a warm human being, a man who understood a young fellow because he's the father of a young lady. He said he thought it sad I should give up so much for a girl who couldn't give up anything. He said that in his opinion it was pathetic when a human being didn't realize he wasn't worth that much to another human being."

Ashen, Anne sat on one of the marble benches.

David joined her on the bench. "But I'm a romanticist, I'm afraid," David said. "My favorite poem is the one by Browning that begins: *Give all to love.* Have you ever read the poem?"

Tears sprang to Anne's eyes, and she heard herself saying to this man something she'd never been able to say to Robert Lund. "I don't care about any of this. I'll sell out! You never asked. If you'd asked, I'd have told you that. I don't want to be bought. In his office, I thought you were buying."

"Actually," David said, "what am I giving up? Just a job and a way of life I didn't like. Incidentally, I have plenty of money. If I have a store and you have a store, do you think they'll be compatible?"

He looked so droll that Anne had to laugh. It felt good to laugh there beside him on the marble bench in the warm sunshine. "What about all those girls?" she asked. "I was shocked, really shocked, when I found out you were dating so many girls. I don't think I'll marry you! I think I'll let you dangle on a string for a while!"

"Oh?" David took a box from his pocket and plucked a ring from it and tossed it up and down. "Competing with millions of dollars," he said, "gives a man an inferiority complex. And you weren't exactly encouraging me, you know, to think that you'd not marry the man. So there was this girl, that girl, another girl."

It was strange, Anne thought. You planned so carefully, after you'd identified and even defined what you wanted. You worked so very busily to bring your plans to fruition. Then, one day, all

171

you had to do was walk into a great, lovely home and smile at a lovely, austere woman to get what you had thought all along you wanted. This faker beside her! Did he think she didn't know how much he was giving up just to sit there tossing that ring up and down as if it were a Blumberg quarter ring for little girls? Of course he was giving up a great deal. He was giving up the big job for which he'd been trained and toward which he'd been working his way since teen-age days. Very well. But those were a lot of dollars she was giving up, too, as well as a great lovely home and an assured position in Santa Fe society. Maybe this man didn't want a Blumberg future, just as she didn't want a Lund future now, but the one was as available to her as the other was to him. So if he was willing to take a chance on her, a girl he didn't actually know, and if she was willing to take a chance on him—

"Have I dangled long enough?" David asked.

Woman-wise, Anne asked, "Don't you honestly think we should wait awhile, David, get to know one another better, make plans?"

"No. The first time I met you, I felt I'd been waiting too many years. Plans! I never planned to come to Santa Fe the first time. I just came."

Loretta came out to the patio. "Chow," she called. She giggled. "Debbie says will you grab the ring and kiss the man and come before her souffle collapses into goo?"

Anne thought exuberantly, warmly, happily, that she was the only sensible creature in a world filled with nuts. She thought she'd make the man wait at least a month or two before she'd let him band her finger for life.

David put the ring on her finger. He smiled. "I'm an expert at guessing ring sizes," he said. "Like it?"

"I think—" Anne said; but that was all she could say. After the kiss she sighed, and then she took David by the hand and led him across the patio to the door. "Will you like living here with three women?" she asked tremulously. "Debbie's decided to finish college here, and Loretta's decided she likes this house just fine."

"Oh, well," David said generously, "when we want to be alone, you can always show me more Indian country."

Cheeks pink, eyes glowing, Anne rushed ahead of him to show Mona the ring and tell her the news.

ADVENTURES OF PINOCCHIO by Carlo Collodi .95
AESOP'S FABLES by Aesop .95
ALICE'S ADVENTURES IN WONDERLAND &
  THROUGH THE LOOKING GLASS by Lewis Carroll .95
AROUND THE WORLD IN 80 DAYS by Jules Verne .95
AUTOBIOGRAPHY OF BENJAMIN FRANKLIN
  by Benjamin Franklin .95
BLACK BEAUTY by Anna Sewell .95
CALL OF THE WILD by Jack London .95
"CAPTAIN COURAGEOUS" by Rudyard Kipling .95
CHRISTMAS CAROL by Charles Dickens .95
EREWHON by Samuel Butler .95
FIRST MEN IN THE MOON by H. G. Wells .95
FRANKENSTEIN by Mary Shelley .95
GREEN MANSIONS by W. H. Hudson .95
HAMLET by William Shakespeare .95
HANS BRINKER; OR, THE SILVER SKATES
  by Mary Mapes Dodge 1.25
HEIDI by Johana Spyri .95
HOUND OF THE BASKERVILLES by A. Conan Doyle .95
INVISIBLE MAN by H. G. Wells .95
ISLAND OF DR. MOREAU by H. G. Wells .95
JFK: A COMPLETE BIOGRAPHY 1917-1963
  by William H. A. Carr .95
JUST SO STORIES by Rudyard Kipling .95
KIDNAPPED by Robert L. Stevenson .95
KING SOLOMON'S MINES by H. Rider Haggard .95
LEGEND OF SLEEPY HOLLOW & OTHER STORIES
  by Washington Irving .95
LOOKING BACKWARD by Edward Bellamy .95
LUCK OF ROARING CAMP & OTHER STORIES
  by Bret Harte .95